SAINT KIMBERLY

~

a novel by Fredrick L. Finch

© 2014

ISBN: 1499240015
ISBN 13: 9781499240016

Dedication

To: my very clever brothers, Ralph and Joe and their wives, Betty Jean and Bobbi

To: my sons, Lane, Greg, and Scott who make me proud and their terrific wives Lisa and Karen

To: My grandchildren, Russell, Taylor, Trey, and Jack and their wives, present and to be, Laura, Samantha, and Lauren. And that clever granddaughter, Violet

To: My fantastic nieces, Teri, Tracy, and Tamra and their significant others Nick and Jim and their mother, Patricia and her Aussie husband, Stephen. And nephew Forest and his wife, Margie

And, as always, my partner for over a half-century, Shirley. I could not do it without you.

Additional thanks are given to the artist, Jack Finch, who created the sketch of St. Kimberly.

The cover art is by the author.

Finally, the fictional home of Kimberly and her kin was the real home of the author in the 1980s.

figure 1: Saint Kimberly

Table of Contents

                                               page

INTRODUCTION · vii

I: 1944 MURIEL COEHN SURVIVES DACHAU · · · · · · · · · · · · · · · · · 1

II: 1944 BRIAN KELLY MEETS PATTON · 11

III: 1946-1957 A WAR BRIDE COMES TO AMERICA · · · · · · · · · · · · 17

IV: 1975 DAN MARRIES THE VIRGIN KATE · · · · · · · · · · · · · · · · · 21

V: 1975 SATAN GETS INVOLVED · 29

VI: 1976 THE DOVE ON THE CRIB · 33

VII: 1982 KIMBERLY GOES TO SCHOOL · 37

VIII: 1976-1991 LIFE IN GLENVIEW, ILLINOIS · · · · · · · · · · · · · · · 47

IX: 1991 KIMBERLY ATTENDS CARMEL CATHOLIC H.S. · · · · · · · · 51

X: 1991 THE CRUSADES AND THE KNIGHTS TEMPLAR · · · · · · · 55

XI: 1991 A FIEND WANTS KIMMY · 61

XII: 1995 KIMBERLY GOES TO COLLEGE · · · · · · · · · · · · · · · · · · · 71

XIII: 1997 THE FIGHT FOR GLORIA'S SOUL · · · · · · · · · · · · · · · · · 81

XIV: 1999 ESCAPE TO A CONVENT · 87

XV: 2001 LEAVING THE CONVENT ·95

XVI: 2002 JACKPOT! THE LOTTERY FUNDS THE MISSIONS · · · ·99

XVII: 2005 PREPARING FOR BATTLE · 119

XVIII: 2006 ANOTHER MIRACLE? · 129

XIX: 2008 THE ELECTIONS · 139

XX: 2009 ARMAGEDDON: A HOLY (?) WAR · · · · · · · · · · · · · · · · 149

XXI: 2009 A VISIT TO THE VATICAN · 159

XXII: 2012 A LANDSLIDE ELECTION · 171

XXIII: 2017 THE K-MISSIONS INDUSTRIES · · · · · · · · · · · · · · · · 183

XXIV: 2017 THE POPE EXPLODES A BOMBSHELL · · · · · · · · · · · 187

XXV: 2018 THE APOCALYPSE · 191

XXVI:2018 NATURAL DISASTERS · 199

XXVII: 2018 BI-COSTAL PROTESTORS · 203

XXVIII: 2018 LUCIFER'S LUNATICS · 205

XXIX: 2019 DRUGS: USERS AND PROVIDERS · · · · · · · · · · · · · · 211

XXX: 2020 ARMAGEDDON · 217

XXXI: 2020 PEACE ON EARTH · 221

Introduction

This book pertains to the presence of physical evil in the world and suggests that it cannot be tolerated but must be ripped out, root and branch, if civilization is to survive. Jesus died for our sins but left the sinners to wreak havoc on the innocent. Hitler and what he created could have been prevented at one point in time but he was allowed to create the monster that nearly swallowed the world. It finally took the sacrifice of lives from many nations and the will to spend anything, dare anything, to end the perversion that was Nazism.

The thesis of this book is that another Child of God is needed to complete the job by putting an end to evil and evildoers who prey on the Godly. This child is imagined in the pages that follow.

God's daughter is modeled on Saint Joan of Arc but Saint Kimberly battles for causes more worthy than an ungrateful Charles the king of France. She tries to eliminate all of the evil that is in the world today. She has come to protect the innocent from the evil one and is assisted in this daunting undertaking by her guardian angels, Gabriel, Michael, Raphael, and Samuel. But, be comforted, she will not end up in the flaming pyre as did Saint Joan.

Jesus died for our sins.
Kimberly took the fight to Satan.

I: 1944

Muriel Cohen Survives Dachau

~

Muriel's father, Israel Cohen, was fond of telling her that they were direct descendants of King David but he did not want to hear any of that nonsense of Jesus being related to David. Israel, or Izzy as he was irreverently known much to his dismay, was an uber-Jew and so successful that he had the notion that his wealth and exalted reputation would keep the ragamuffins (as he called Hitler's minions) from his door. Rabbi Cohen was well-known in Munich and highly respected in his community. This would later prove to be his undoing and lead to unfortunate ends among his family.

Dachau was only nine miles away and, when the camp opened in August, 1935 it took only a year of so before the SS began sending Jehovah's Witnesses, homosexuals, and emigrants to his hell-hole. In 1938, 11,000 Austrian Jews were forced into this camp.

Israel Cohen, his wife Hannah, and Muriel were among those rounded up and soon were at the iron gates looking at the motto, "Arbeit macht frei." Since German was their native language they read, "work will make you free" but they strongly feared that freedom was not in their immediate future.

Israel and Hannah were immediately sent to the crematorium. Whether Muriel was more or less fortunate could be debated but she survived because she caught the eye of the camp commandant who used her most cruelly. He debased her, but could not break her spirit which she kept hidden deep inside as she endured.

After a year or so, she was tossed aside to be replaced by a new plaything that came in on yesterday's train. At least her ordeal had saved her from starvation but the starving times were just beginning. Her new home was a hell-hole barracks, dirty, smelly and filled with misery and the low mutterings of those in physical and mental agony. They had learned what true evil was and Nazism was bringing Hell on earth to six million Jews and many others. If Hitler was not the Spawn of Satan then he certainly was his accomplice. One knows with absolute certainty one inhabitant of Hell and Adolph is he.

Muriel had endured her interludes with her tormentor by retreating into her inner core to write psalms in her head. In the barracks, she encountered an emaciated creature in rags who shocked and surprised Muriel by greeting her with a smile. "I am Sister Margaret." she said. "I no longer have any remnants of the habit of my order but am fashionably dressed in scraps like the rest of the visitors in this delightful place."

Muriel was stunned by such commonplace banter in a place where one only heard hate and rage against God and man. It took time but Muriel was brought around and eventually developed enough interest in things outside of her seething spirit to ask Sister Margaret about the necklace, if that was what it was, that she continuously played with when there were no guards prowling around. Not only did they prowl but, from time to time, dragged one of the less skeletal women outside for their fiendish purposes. No longer did anyone protest or struggle. It was just inevitable so let be what was to be.

The "necklace" turned out to be what Maggie (Sister Margaret was a bit formal for the circumstances) called a circular "Rosary" fashioned out of peas, beans, and scraps of wood held together by a ragged string that Maggie had to replace frequently. Over time, Maggie explained the complicated structure of the Rosary. The beans and peas would ordinarily be replaced by wooden beads, pearls, precious stones, or any material that could be fashioned into a ball and pierced to hold a cord, chain, or whatever.

There was little to entertain them so Maggie, the nun, taught Muriel, the Jew, the function of the Rosary. Fashioned in a circle, it began with a cross on which one would say the Apostles Creed after making the Sign of the Cross. Then, on the bean, one said the "Our Father" followed by three "Hail Marys" on the three peas which came next on the string and the "Glory Be". Of course all of these prayers and phrases had to be explained but all became familiar and memorized by Muriel over time. Then came another bean followed by ten peas. There were five sets of these. On each bean one started with a meditation on one of the "mysteries." (Five per Rosary, in groups categorized as "Joyful", "Sorrowful", "Glorious", or "Luminous.") After the Mystery, One "Our Father" (the bean) and ten "Hail Marys" (the peas) were said followed by the "Glory Be." Then the second mystery was stated and briefly meditated upon followed by "Our Father", ten "Hail Marys", and the "Glory be." This continued on around until the person saying the Rosary came all the way back to the second bean where concluding prayers were said.

Muriel decided that the recitation of the Rosary was much like a Hindu mantra that was repetitiously chanted or sung until the incantation moved the mind to some peaceful place. Maggie did not mind this characterization and the recitation of the Rosary became a source of comfort to Muriel in an otherwise awful place. All one's will and creativity was required to just stay alive and to endure the many and impossible tasks they were given so the distraction of the Rosary was a very good thing, indeed.

Muriel asked Maggie if the church allowed them to "worship graven images" as is forbidden in Jewish tradition. The young nun explained,

"Remember that our tradition is very, very, old. Many of our worshipers were illiterate and the beautiful statues and paintings were instructional aids. They told a story and, because they were a tribute to all that is holy, we made them as beautiful as humanly possible. The greatest artists and artisans of the day were supported, and sometimes involuntarily drafted, by powerful Popes and Princes. That is how the Sistine Chapel came to be. Michelangelo did not really enjoy this backbreaking job but the Pope pretty much forced him to do it."

"Anyway, we do not worship a beautiful statue of the Virgin Mary or St. Michael the Archangel but they provide a physical symbol to focus upon as we think about them, say a prayer, or just enjoy the beauty of the creator's work."

On the way to the day's 14-hour shift at the factory where prisoners were deliberately worked to death, Maggie found a broken piece of band-saw blade that she smuggled back to the barracks. Over time, she cut a slice on the back corner of the post supporting the shelves upon which they lived, slept, and died. The removable edge was about 3 X 3 inches and Maggie then burrowed into the wood to create a niche about six inches deep and two wide. Into this hidey-hole went her precious rosary and Muriel's treasure. This was a very fine opal, about the size of a quarter, that was concealed during her time with Herr Komandant in ways that do not bear thinking about. It was repeatedly swallowed, retrieved, washed, and then swallowed again. Are you not sorry you asked? Anyway, she now had a place to hide it.

Many years after liberation, an old lady named Muriel returned as a tourist and retrieved both the opal and the homemade rosary from where they had remained concealed for many years.

Satan knew the future and, often, there was little that he could do to change it but he tried. Oh, how he tried! "Baal! Go get me Hans Krause from his place in the lake of molten lava."

"Hans? the serial killer of women and children?"

"Yes, That very one."

Hans Krause (number 552, there were many of them) was retrieved from the flames and dropped into a vat of ice and water to cool off. The ice was as painful on his burns as the fire had been; this was Hell, you know. The Devil said, "Hans, I have a little job for you. I am sending you back to the Germany of five years ago. You are to join the newly formed Nazi party and work your way into Hitler's elite SS (Schutzstaffel, or defense corps) and thence into the Waffen SS that is assigned to the Dachau Concentration Camp. I will handle the details to get you there."

"Once there, you will go to Barracks 500 and retrieve from space 500-36 one Muriel Cohen. You will then take her to some isolated place, assault her, and kill her. I know that you are good at this so get to it. When you return you will be rewarded."

When Hans left, Satan explained to his pal Baal (sometimes called, in the Bible, Beelzebub) that Muriel was the be the mother of the mother of a child that would cause them no end of trouble. So, he would try to snuff out the whole line. He knew that it was a long shot because his adversary had beaten him too often before.

And so, it came to pass that, in the dark of the night years later, Muriel was roughly dragged from her bunk, thrown over Hans' shoulder, and carried outside. His fellow guards winked and grinned as they saw one of their pals carrying off yet another helpless woman for his own purposes.

When they entered the empty shower room, Hans tossed the terrified Muriel into a corner and started undoing his belt. He felt, and then saw, a brilliant light behind him and turned to see Samuel, the archangel, in full-dress mode from his white wings, to his golden armor, to, especially, his flaming sword that was pressed into Hans' chest, backing him up against the cinder-block wall.

Samuel looked over at Muriel and said, "Go back to your bunk without fear of the guards between here and there. They are all asleep. You will be at peace and fall asleep without remembering anything that happened tonight."

After Muriel departed, Samuel said to Hans, "You, my little friend, are on your way back to Hell from whence you came."

Maggie was surprised and relieved to see Muriel return so quickly but she did not ask any questions. The next day, the camp rumor mill was buzzing about the guard who had hung himself in the showers with his own suspenders. After several days, the fact that he had left a suicide note saying that he could no longer live with the things that he had done surfaced. Maggie thought, "A-Ha!" But she said nothing and neither did Muriel.

When Hans was dropped back in front of Lucifer's throne, he tried to stammer out his excuses and explanations but the King of the Underworld would have none of it. He just sent Hans back to his lake of boiling lava. Hans hoped that "forever" was not quite the same as "eternity" and the damned took some solace in the rumor that, after sufficient suffering and atonement, they would be allowed to enter the outskirts of Heaven as probationary members. He was, after all, a merciful God, was he not?

Back at Dachau, Maggie and Muriel continued to endure what they had to endure and just tried to survive each day.

While the nun told Muriel about the New Testament, Muriel explained the Torah to Maggie. At least, as much as could be remembered about this huge body of work. Jews believe that Moses brought down from Mount Sinai not only the Ten Commandments but the original books of the Torah which provided, among other things, wisdom for living. Over time, Jews added the writings of the prophets and history of the people. In the second century, a gathering of Rabbis attempted to document and explain this large this huge body of work in sort of an instruction guide called the Talmud.

One rabbi stated that if one attempted to read one page of the Talmud a day, it would take seven years to complete the task.

Muriel began to weave Catholic prayers and New Testament homilies among her psalms and eventually came up with a mental equivalent of a book of poetry whose theme was how to live in peace and joy among the wreckage of a living hell. The spirit was willing but the flesh was weak and Maggie was nearing death when America arrived to save those who were salvageable.

When the troops liberated Dachau on April 29, 1945, General Felix Sparks did not try very hard to keep outraged soldiers from assassinating German guards hiding among the pitiful prisoners that they had, only yesterday, been tormenting. Sergeant Brian Kelly was one of many who took it upon himself to avenge those unable to get their own richly deserved revenge. When the politically correct rear echelon M-F's tried to make a big deal of this happening, General Patton dismissed all charges against Sparks and his men. While he made no comment, it can be assumed that Patton most likely approved of the on-site administration of justice. When German civilians routinely denied any complicity in what went on in nearby prison camps, Patton is said to have asked, "Just who the hell do they think did all of this? The Eskimos?"

II: 1944

Brian Kelly Meets Patton:

~

Brian was one of the the millions of American soldiers who rushed in to rid the world of the plague of hate spread by the complicit spawn of Hitler. After they were defeated, the German people claimed no knowledge of what was happening while it was happening and would have us believe that they were not complicit in any of the goings on that occurred. Brian Kelly hated the "gnat-zees" even before he ran up against them and afterward hated them in ways that went way beyond hate.

Somewhere in Sicily, Brian's foxhole buddy, Bud, peeks out of the hole and quickly ducks back as a mortar shell explodes somewhere way too close. "Geez! Bri! Our one and last hope is to know that Jesus will come again soon."

"He can't come too soon to suit me." Said Brian as he shifted his chaw from one cheek to the other and spits before saying, "But when he sees what I am seeing, he will be mightily pissed!" Rising up he takes a couple of quick shots and permanently ends the military career of another German who foolishly tried to rush a sharpshooter's lair.

When General Patton slapped a soldier suffering from what was then called "shell shock," he nearly ended his own career and he also pulled Corporal Kelly off the front lines to carry his bags to his next assignment which just happened to be an ass-chewing by General Dwight David Eisenhower.

General Ike was fed up with Patton's insubordinate ways. The man just could not be controlled and seemed to forget that Dwight no longer reported to him as he once had. The five-star Supreme Commander of the Allied Forces in Europe exiled Patton to an imaginary base across from French Cherbourg where he presided over a phantom army consisting of blown up (as in balloons, not exploded) tanks and trucks and papier-mâché' cannons and cardboard barracks. The Nazis were convinced that since Patton was the most aggressive tactical genius the U.S. Army had, and the one who who beat Rommel in Africa, he would be the natural leader of any invasion force. They believed that Patton was the most capable fighting General that the Allies had. And so they kept their eyes on Patton and not on the beaches of Normandy. On D-Day, June 6, 1944; Hitler refused to believe that the invasion "was the real thing" because the feared Patton and his troops had not yet departed. Unfortunately, Brian had been promoted to Sergeant and sent off to join the fun on Omaha Beach.

During the Civil War, going into battle was to "see the elephant." Well, Brian had seen the elephant, the hippopotamus, and the mongoose. He also managed to join up with Patton later as the fighting General raced to relieve the troops near Bastogne in a serious fight called "the Battle of the Bulge." Even today, visitors to Bastogne can see an American Sherman tank in the town square beside the bronze bust of General Anthony McAuliffe whose one word response to a German demand that he surrender was, "Nuts!."

After the Germans had been defeated, the American soldiers grew tired of waiting for orders to return "home" and they began singing,

"Oh. Harry Truman, why can't we go home? We have conquered Italy and we have conquered Rome! Now that we have beat the Master Race, why can't you find shipping space? For us, Harry Truoooman! Why can't we go home?"

Brian Kelly was going nowhere. He had a postwar job in an Army warehouse sorting German equipment for reuse by the bombed-out citizens of Germany who had nothing. No food. No clothes. No heat or shelter. Nothing! Young women had one commodity and American soldiers had plenty of Hershey bars.

But the skinny Muriel Cohen had survived worse and, through luck and pluck, managed to get a job in a warehouse sorting shoes and boots into pairs and then into sizes prior to distribution to the pitiful ones living in the rubble that was once Munich. She had food, a single room with a cot and a semi-wrecked fireplace that she kept going with shards and splinters that came from once-magnificent homes. In brief, she was in heaven.

Little did Muriel know that her proposed marriage to Lt. Kelly had been rejected by the paper pushers who had the authority to say no to everything and no authority to say yes to anything. Unfortunately for these rear echelon weenies, Georgie Patton got wind of the situation and fired off his usual tactful memo.

TO: Supreme Headquarters Allied
Expeditionary Force (SHAEF)
FROM: General George Patton
SUBECT: The Honorable State of
Marriage

It has come to my attention that some draft-dodging pencil pusher in your HQ has denied the request of Lt. Brian Kelly to marry the lovely and patriotic Muriel Cohen (Lately of Munich, by way of Dachau). She has worked for the Third Army in a sensitive capacity and has earned all the appropriate clearances required for her work.

Lt. Kelly served under me with great distinction as we tricked the Germans into thinking the invasion was coming from where it was not. To his credit, he then volunteered to go ashore on D-Day and not only survived but earned a Bronze Medal, Purple Heart, and a battlefield commission from yours truly.

I, personally, would take it to be a great favor if you would get off your comfortable asses and give this brave soldier all of the paper that is needed to wed and immediately transport both to the Unites States in an expeditious manner.

cc: General Dwight Eisenhower

General Eisenhower annotated the memo as follows: "Boys, If you know what is good for you, you will get this done ASAP....Ike"

III: 1946-1957

A War Bride Comes to America

~

A lonely soldier and a beautiful, if somewhat thin (emaciated might be a better word) young lady did what young ones always do and soon another war bride was on a steamer heading across the Atlantic to meet her soldier boy. He had walked right by her in Dachau as he shot a few camp guards. She, on the other hand was busy in the process of getting saved from the horrors she had endured. They had passed by unaware of each other but they were fated to meet later beside a very large pile of war-surplus bedroom slippers.

On the boat, Muriel filled several school tablets with the poems, prayers, and songs that had been written in her mind as she survived what was going on outside on her body. After a joyful reunion at quayside, Brian went to college on the G.I. Bill which was a brilliant solution to the problem of what to do with hordes of young men returning from learning to kill or be killed and now ready to get what they had longed for as they struggled to survive and prevail. What did they want? Women and jobs! And the priority varied from day to day. In the meantime, women, Rosie the riveters, and others, were used to jobs and wages. So the Government mounted a propaganda blitz designed to convince them to return to the kitchen and enter into a state of married bliss, in no particular order. It worked out pretty well and soon thousands of young men were well-educated and working while the "Baby Boom" was begun. Except for the "duck and cover" drills in schools it was a fairly blissful period in America's history. But, nothing is perfect and the threat of thermonuclear war and segregation were a problem to be worked on.

While Brian worked toward a degree as a pharmacist, Muriel wrote, rewrote, and polished her essays, poems, and whatever to the point where it was very publishable. It was accepted by Scott, Foresman, and Company and this is how they came to end up in Glenview, IL, the home of that notable publisher. Muriel's "Dachau Devotionals" never would match SF & Co.'s "Dick and Jane" series of children's readers but it did stand up to "The Diary of Anne Frank" as another testament of the fortitude and optimism of young women.

After graduation, Brian soon bought a drug store near the railway station and obtained a G.I. loan for a modest home a few blocks away at 2141 Fir Street. Kate Kelly was born in 1954 and grew up in unremarkable ways in a pleasant little village on the outskirts of Chicago.

Muriel had a modest period of small-time celebrity but her book tended to continuously renew itself as it was discovered and rediscovered from generation to generation. In this way, young jewish girls learned about the horrors of the holocaust and young Catholic girls came identify with the heroic Maggie the nun.

Making "folk art" rosaries out of peas and beans from time-to-time became a hobby in parochial schools. Making crosses, baskets, and stuff from the palm fronds of Palm Sunday was another thing that most Catholic schoolgirls were quite skilled at.

The adolescent Kate usually was able to remain unassociated with Muriel Cohen's well known book and worked very hard to keep it so. In contrast, she reveled in her special status as the daughter of "Doc" Kelly as it gave her all sorts of perks and bennies at the soda fountain that was part of the drug store.

Kate endured, nay, reveled in Catholic grade school, high school, and college, and knew as much about the saints and Catholic dogma as the Pope. At times, it seemed that she enjoyed them more. Her young life prepared her for what she was destined to become and no one would have been less likely to guess what that was than she.

IV: 1975

Dan Marries the Virgin Kate

~

Dan Ryan came from a long line of Irish immigrants and his father, Paddy, progressed from Pullman Porter, to railroad tycoon, to the founder of ZIPLINE, a strong competitor to FedEx and UPS. Paddy was happy that Kate's father was an Irishman and a decorated war hero named Brian Kelly but was less sure about Muriel Cohen Kelly. Could a converted Jew be counted upon? Time would tell. Their son, Danny Ryan was all set to marry the beautiful and pious Kate Kelly. The miraculous granddaughter, Kimberly Ryan was not yet a consideration.

Because her parents were off to see Grandma Muriel and Grandpa Brian, Kate was home alone surrounded by wedding magazines and daydreaming of the day that she and Dan would be married. They had gone to school together at OLPH but did not become a couple, or even become aware of each other until they happened to sit together on a bus trip to Washington D.C. to support the right to life movement. During the trip, they discovered how much they had in common and began to date when they left OLPH for Carmel Catholic High School in Mundelein, IL.

They decided early on to maintain a chaste and celibate relationship but nevertheless were very much in love and remained so after graduation and during four years apart when he went off to Notre Dame and she to the Loyola University of Chicago.

They returned to Glenview after graduation and, each living at home, joined the throng of commuters at the beautiful suburban train station each morning to their jobs in downtown Chicago. Dan had snagged a job at the Board of Trade and Kate was an apprentice accountant at the giant firm of Wallingford and Buckley.

They still lived with their parents but had amassed a nest egg of sufficient size for a down payment on a condo near the train station. Celibacy was all very fine in theory but hugging and kissing only went so far. Kate would get "all tingly" thinking about the legally and morally permissible, even mandatory, activities sanctioned by the sacrament of matrimony. It was in this state of mind that she answered the doorbell

Standing there was a interesting looking little man in a brown suit and a derby hat. He had a five-o'clock shadow and, in general, looked like someone's bookie. But he had a pleasant voice and asked, "May I come in and talk to you a bit, Kate?"

Kate was horrified when she heard herself invite this total stranger into the house but, for some strange reason, she was certain that he would do her no harm. In fact, she found that she was looking forward to talking to him.

He invited himself to have a seat in Dad's favorite rocker and said, "I know that this seems strange but I promise you that it is far less weird than that night when the angel appeared to the blessed Mary. My name is Samuel. You might remember that it was Gabriel who appeared to Mary and Michael whose main job is to war upon Satan. And, Raphael whose name means "God heals. In fact, the names of most angels end with the suffix, -el."

"Samuel, hum...el? Is this some kind of a hint?" Asked Kate. "Are you telling me that you are an angel? For some reason I am kinda prepared to believe it."

"Well, yes. You know this because you are prepared to receive the message. That is the way that angels work. We are messengers. That is what angels do. Among other things, of course. But, since we are going to be friends, call me Sammy."

"Get to it then." Said Kate. "Why are you here and what's up?"

"First, lets say a little prayer together. You know this one...

"Hail Mary, full of grace, the Lord is with thee. Blessed are thou among women and blessed is the fruit of thy womb, Jesus. Holy Mary, mother of God, pray for us sinners now and at the hour of our death."

Kate followed along and, with eyes wide, said, "Did you come to tell me that I am going to die!?"

"Nope," said Samuel, "The other thing."

"What other thing?"

"The ...blessed is the fruit of thy womb thing."

"That can't be, Sammy! I am engaged and still a virgin!"

"So was Mary and she accepted God's will, with grace, shall we say?

"To cut to the chase, Kate, the Armageddon is coming and the child of God is needed again. But, this time, it will be the Daughter of God, the sister of the Son of God. And you will be the mother. The Jesuits at Loyola gave you the preparation needed but the hard work will fall upon the daughter. "

Seeing that Kate was about to stroke out, Samuel offered the only reassurance that he could. "Kate, I know that this news from some old guy in a three-piece suit is tough to take but let me present my bona fides, so to speak. Brace yourself! Here comes the full-court angel aspect."

And, with that, an incandescent being appeared in the middle of the suburban living room. Gone was the unshaven guy in scuffed shoes and there was a magnificent glowing being complete with golden breastplate, tunic, sandals, and snow-white wings that almost reached from wall to wall. There also was, of course, the requisite halo. In a voice like a heavenly chorus, Samuel said, "Does this help? This is a very big deal and my formal persona might be more suitable for the occasion."

Kate murmured, "So be it Samuel. I cannot refuse and I will do my best knowing that God will be with me. But, we still have the problem that Mary had. Gabriel convinced Joseph that the deal was legitimate but what about Dan?"

"No problems, Kate. That has already been taken care of. When he arrives for your dinner date tonight, he will come bearing an armful of red roses and a full understanding of his role in this glorious undertaking."

"What about the biology of the thing, Sammy?"

"Even now, your own egg is dividing after being fertilized by the power of the Holy Spirit rather than a spermatozoon. The zygote is growing and will produce a beautiful and powerful daughter in the natural course of events."

"So, it is kinda a done deal?"

"Yep. You and Dan will be given the graces and knowledge to raise her up to be what she must be. And, like Saint Joan, she will be a mighty warrior in the fight against Lucifer and his army of evil. The Final Battle is coming and the times will be troubling but Saint Kimberly will prevail against the forces of Beelzebub."

"Saint Kimberly? Where did THAT come from?"

"Well, Kate, that was the name you picked out later on in your pregnancy. Kimberly, Kim, Kimmie, and her high school chums will call her 'the Kimster.' We angels can see ahead in time and know what is to be and that was the name you will pick but have not yet done so."

"I must admit that I kinda like it. But is that any name for the child of God?"

"There is no wrong name. Excuse me, can I return to my informal aspect? These wings are sort of awkward and I would like to sit for a spell and smoke my cigar."

"Angels don't smoke cigars! Besides, cigars stink!"

"Not heavenly cigars. They will remind you of the incense after a high mass. Besides, it will give me something to do with my hands and make me seem more human."

"Go ahead! I have gotten in too deep to let a little Holy Smoke bother me."

And so, Sammy and Kate spent a very pleasant and highly informative afternoon discussing what was to be. She with her Diet Coke and he with his see-gar. Of course, angels don't tell all and some things were meant to be discovered rather than revealed. Sammy hinted that, after 2,000 years, the message of peace and love had not managed to protect the innocent from evildoers so might not

God decide to try a different approach? More, Old Testament, shall we say? In a David and Goliath kind of way. Or like Sodom and Gomorrah but on a more individual level.

V: 1975

Satan Gets Involved

~

Meanwhile, somewhere in the metaphorical "down below" Satan looks "up" from his throne and wonders what has just happened to disturb the equilibrium that was beginning to form. Another child has been born to the enemy. Lucifer had a battle coming up and his rebel army was growing in strength after having fed on lost souls for over 2,000 years.

The King of the Underworld thinks, "This will bear watching! Eventually I will have to do something about this. My opponent is cunning and moves in mysterious ways; but, a daughter?"

"When she goes to school I will place one of my minions nearby to watch for an opportunity to corrupt or destroy her. I could not tempt her brother but she is a mere female and I have had good luck with them, beginning with Eve. Salome and Delilah also worked out pretty well for me."

Beelzebub creates Clete and Gloria and puts them in Kimberly's path. One will try to seduce her and the other will try to kill her. Among Kim's other enemies were Sister Fortuna and the entire leadership of Abu Nidal, Hezbollah, Al-Qaeda, and their surrogates.

There are undoubtably good Muslims and followers of Islam but few are willing to speak out in support of Christians and the United States. Some claim to be "Children of the Book" following in the tradition of Jews and Christians but, from Saladin to Mahmoud Ahmadinejad (President of Iran from 2005-2013), they do not seem to like Christians or westerners very much. More than a few were very useful tools in the service of "The Great Deceiver." Those who flew jets full of passengers into New York's tallest buildings undoubtably had the Devil in the cockpit with them.

Satan found willing helpers in his war against Christianity in the Middle East. Proponents of a jihad, or "Holy War" had the fanatical notion, nay, delusion, that they could establish a world-wide Caliphate against the civilized world to the north of them. It is easy for the unwashed and illiterate to inflame those similarly deprived of intellect and material goods.

The King of Trickery had an ace in the hole in the form of the orphan girl Molly that he had been grooming to plant as a nun in the school that the as-yet unborn Kimberly would attend. And yes, that old Debbel could see into the future but God had blinded him with an inability to know how things would turn out. And, considering his opponent, they usually turned out badly. "Curses, foiled again!" was Satan's most frequently used euphemism.

In any event, Lucifer managed to ensure that Molly traveled the same commuter train from Chicago to Glenview that Dan used. Over time, they became acquainted and Molly always took any empty seat that happened to be next to Dan. Being human, and a mere man, Dan was flattered that this exotic brunette seemed to enjoy his company and, when summer came with the seasonal shedding of heavy outer clothing, Dan was deliciously uncomfortable by all of Molly's charms which were on parade right next to him. While Sammy was giving Kate the joyous news, Molly was telling Dan that she had a "sweet little apartment" very near the train station and perhaps he might want to drop in for a quickie. "Oh, excuse me," she said, to add the exclamation point, "I did not mean that kind of a quickie. Oh, dear no. I meant some of the homemade lemonade that I am quite expert at making. Think it over, we have all summer and waiting will make it all the sweeter...The lemonade, I mean. Well, here is our stop. See you tomorrow?"

Dan almost skipped down the sidewalk home and the last thing that he expected to encounter before he reached his trusting bride-to-be was an angel ready to fill him in on the blessed event ..."Really BLESSED, if you get my point!" Said Sammy. Pow! All thoughts of carnal adventures with some random lady on a train vanished, never to return, as Samuel filled him on on the whats-what. Dan started leaving home a little earlier and returning a little later which really impressed his boss but left Molly waiting at the station, so to speak.

VI: 1976

The Dove on the Crib

~

In the fullness of time, Kate gives birth. When the nurse brings Baby Kimberly to her, she remarks on the two doves that have stood vigil on the window sill for the last hour.

"I have never seen such interesting doves." The nurse says. "They are the whitest things I have ever seen and those strange red markings of their breast look a little like a cross. Well, they will get on with their bird work sooner or later. There is not much to eat around this hospital."

The nurse was right. The doves left when Kim and Kate went home but showed up in the crabapple tree in the back yard of their Glenview home at 2141 Fir. Dan and Kate had "inherited" the family home when Brian and Muriel departed for a smaller house on a golf course in a village called Golf, IL.

Back on Fir street, the doves nested and brought forth a brood of hatchlings that bred true. Thus, they were a new species that maintained their distinctive coloring and markings.

Uncle Ben, who was a veterinarian and knew about such things, named them "the Templar Dove" because the curious markings on their breast resembled the red cross worn on the tunics of the Knights Templar. Ben built a cote that the pigeons found hospitable and he managed to pluck an egg or two from each nest which he incubated until he had a fairly large collection of these beautiful birds in several nesting boxes scattered around the county. He also managed to get them listed on the rolls of "threatened species" so that they would be protected.

Whenever Kimmie was allowed to toddle around in the back yard, the doves would follow her because they had imprinted on her from the time they were nestlings. She grew up with the doves and their interactions were such that parents, relatives, and even strangers remarked on the relationship between bird and child. Kimmie never knew anything different and saw nothing unusual about having a dove on each shoulder as she wandered to and fro in the safety of her grassy yard.

Kimmie never knew the joys of a pet cat or dog. With the doves hanging around, having these sort of animals would not be prudent. But, she did not miss them. She had her doves.

Clever Uncle Ben enlisted the help of another occasional relative, "Uncle Sammy" to build several heated roosts that kept the doves warm and cosy during the fierce Chicago winters. And so, the birds grew and multiplied and Ben ended up in the bird-by-mail business. Everyone wanted a pair of these beautiful birds because they were especially friendly and seemed to want to be around humans.

Beelzebub kept watch from time-to-time (he had a short attention span and an infinite amount of time) and, one day, he saw Kate kiss Kimmy saying, "I will be right back sweetie. I have to go next door to borrow a cup of beans from Mrs. Owens."

A chance! Quick as a wink, Beelzebub dashed into the park, grabbed a rabbit and returned to show this furry treasure to the toddler wandering alone around the back yard. As he approached the back gate, the Archangel Raphael appeared. "Who are you?" the evil one shouted even though he knew the answer.

"I am the babysitter today. You had best be on your way to avoid trouble."

And, The Evil One did. He had, after all, all the time in the world.

When Kate returned, Kimmie ran up and hugged her leg saying, "Mummy, If you love the doves, the doves will love you."

"Yes, dear. We must all love each other. Raphael, Was Kim any problem today?"

"No, Kate. That little sweetie will always have her guardian angels hanging around to keep an eye on things. Well, I'll be getting about my business. I'll be around if I am needed."

VII: 1982

Kimberly Goes to School

~

When she came of age, Kim entered school like any other American child. Her parents enrolled her at the Catholic school for the Our Lady of Perpetual Help parish. Commonly known as OLPH among the adults and "old lady pickle head" by mischievous children, OLPH's church was designed in a beautiful Georgian revival style, vaguely reminiscent of Thomas Jefferson's Monticello. As she grew older, the only thing that always bothered Kim was the gold-gilded Christ on the cross over the altar. Somehow, it did not seem seemly.

The school was rather basic in the way that most parish schools are but the dedication and example of the few nuns that remained created an atmosphere of respect for achievement and appreciation of fundamental values. Kimmie cheerfully toiled away in this environment and grew in knowledge and faith. She also learned social graces and soon became, and remained, popular with students and staff. Except, that is, for Sister Fortuna and the custodian, Clete. Without their knowledge, they had been recruited by the Master of the Underworld. They would later follow Kim by transferring to her high school.

Sister Fortuna had been selected and guided since she was a mere ragamuffin to present a respectable outward appearance very much in contrast to her baser inner instincts. Satan had chosen her for the long-term mission of leading Kim astray or destroying her entirely.

Molly, as the child who would later become Sister Fortuna was called, lied, cheated, and stole and would rather harm small animals than pet them. As she grew out of childhood, her capabilities increased and she made a very good living swindling what she called "the poor fools who were put on earth to be fleeced by me." Molly soon was ensnared in so many scandals and failed cons that she decided to retreat to a nearby convent to lie low and regroup. This decision was guided by an unknown force of which Molly was not aware. Molly also had a few social diseases that needed time and medication to heal. Each step of her sorry life had been programmed by the Evil One but Molly was completely unaware of the extent to which she was the creature of The Devil and his underlings. And so, Sister Fortuna was born and, after having served a lengthy sentence in the nunnery, was turned loose on the helpless children of OLPH. Arranging her assignment as a teacher had required all of old Beelzebub's considerable assets and skills but it had been done and Sister Fortuna was to become the bane of Kimberly's existence.

But, other forces had made Sister Mary Grace the Mother Superior of the OLPH nun's house and Principal of the school. Neither knew how they came to become engaged in some sort of Catholic Mexican standoff or even that it was going on but Sister Mary Grace kept Sister Fortuna from wreaking too much havoc upon Kim's ego and opportunities.

The lamb may have followed Mary to school one day but Kim's doves were always there. A pair nested in the trees by the creek bordering the playground and they liked to circle high above Kim any time that she was at play. Any unfortunate child who tried to pick on Kim found that they had to endure a pecking by a dove on each shoulder or a dive-bombing that painfully relieved them of their hair if bareheaded or of their hat if one was worn. The children soon came to accept this strange circumstance as a normal part of life around Kimmie. Children are nothing if not adaptable.

At the time of her First Communion, Kim noticed a couple of pinpricks of blood on the palms of her hands but the tiny dots on her rib and feet went unnoticed. Too young and inexperienced to recognize stigmata, this phenomenon went unnoticed amid the excitement of the day.

Kimmie did all of the things that elementary school children do except that she exceeded all expectations, both social and academic. Of course, her teachers admired her but, surprisingly, so did the other children. Her special friend, Gloria Costello, had the misfortune to be the friend that was selected by the forces of darkness to betray Kim.

Clete, the custodian, was doing his best to corrupt Kim but, handsome as he was, she was not having any of his suggestive offers of "friendship" and, in fact, was too innocent to even take note of it. In desperation, Clete took to placing pornographic novels in her locker but Kim just tossed them in the trash can after a disinterested glance. Clete usually retrieved them but one was found by Sister Mary Grace who asked Clete, the trusted custodian, to help her "keep an eye out for the pervert" who was using the school's trash to discard his "filth." This shook up Clete and he backed away from this strategy. Not, however, before Sister Fortuna had found a couple of these depraved samples of erotica and used them for her own entertainment and enlightenment. Fortuna hated her descent into depravity but was so besotted with the entrapments that the Devil provided that she could not escape nor did she want to.

As they wound their innocent way toward the time of their rite of Confirmation, Kim grew in piety as Gloria was led and indoctrinated along less wholesome paths. Sister Fortuna encouraged an unwholesome friendship with too much hugging, patting and, surreptitiously, the occasional slow kiss along with the recounting of mischievous "pranks" that became ever more cruel as Gloria was desensitized to the immorality involved with these capers.

By the time of their Confirmation in the ninth grade, Gloria was able to participate in the ritual but without any appreciation of it. When they participated in the rite of confession, or "reconciliation," the priest was tolerant of Kim's recapitulation of trite transgressions and bored by Gloria's completely imaginary list of "sins."

Father Lorenzo recognized the essential nature of Kimberly and, by the grace of God, had a vague idea that this child was to become something special. When she came to him asking for information about the "special gifts" or graces associated with Confirmation, he sent her to the internet and asked her to report back. She did. And, the next day, presented the following information in nicely typed form.

Wikipedia states that the Catechism
of the Catholic Church lists the
seven gifts as follows:

* wisdom: is the capacity to love
  spiritual things more than
  material ones;

* understanding: in understanding,
  we comprehend how we need to live
  as followers of Christ.

* counsel (right judgment): with the
  gift of counsel/right judgment,
  we know the difference between
  right and wrong, and we choose to
  do what is right.

* fortitude (courage): with the gift
  of fortitude/courage, we overcome
  our fear and are willing to
  take risks as a follower of
  Jesus Christ.

* knowledge: with the gift of
  knowledge, we understand
  the meaning of God. The gift
  of knowledge is more than an
  accumulation of facts;

* piety (reverence): with the gift of
  reverence, sometimes called piety,
  we have a deep sense of respect for
  God and the Church.

* fear of the Lord (wonder and awe):
  with the gift of fear of the Lord
  we are aware of the glory and
  majesty of God.

During the Confirmation mass, Kim again noticed the stigmata present at her First Communion but, this time she recognized it for what it was. Her collection of "holy cards" listed stigmata as occurring to many saints, among them St. Francis of Assisi, St. Catherine of Siena, St. Clare of Montefalco, and dozens, if not hundreds of others.

After the mass, she called Father Lorenzo aside and showed him her palms asking, "Father. What do I do about this? I had the same marks at the time of my First Communion but thought nothing of it."

"Kimmie, there is nothing to do but wait to see what it is all about. I suspect that it means that something quite special will come of your life but you have to live it one day at a time and do your best, with what you have, where you are. God gives us what we need, when we need it, and so it will be with you. I am going to ask Sister Mary to talk with you about the religious life and see whether this sort of vocation might be a path for you to follow."

While Sister Mary talked to and guided Kimmie, one of the other teachers had befriended Gloria. The two girls were best pals but did not talk about their friendships with their different nunfriends. Also left unsaid in their conversations was any mention of tortured animals or waylaid classmates but Gloria was a master of sociopathy and, like many of her ilk, was able to deceive Kimberly and maintain a long-term friendship. But her main friendship was with Sister Fortuna and carried out in hidden nooks and crannies around the school.

While Gloria was experimenting with forbidden fruit, Kim was exploring fruit toppings on sundaes as a "soda jerk" at Grandpa Brian's drug store. She enjoyed working after school and she was given a short menu of "freebies" that she could pass out to friends. Obviously, everyone wanted to be her friend but Kimmie wisely kept a checklist, actually a clever person-by-treat chart, that listed who got what, and when. In that way, no one felt cheated, favored, or disrespected.

One regular habitué of the sandwich shop booths was "old Gabe" who barely avoided hobo status by ordering grilled cheese and Dr. Pepper three times a day. He dressed plainly but was clean and always polite and never "creepy" around the young girls who hung out with Kimmie. No one knew, or much cared, where he lived. He was just always around.

And, fortunately, Gabe was there when a gun-man tried to rob the snack bar. Avoiding, against all reason, the main cash register. The madman tried to shoot up the gaggle of girls, and, especially, Kim, but his AK-47 jammed and "Old Gabe" laid him low with a roundhouse swing to his head. He later told the police who hauled the gunman off that he was a retired Green Beret and this little action was not a big deal.

And so, the Archangels, Gabriel, Raphael, and Samuel, had had their turn but Michael had yet to show up for his big appearance.

VIII: 1976-1991

Life in Glenview, Illinois

~

Her twin brothers, Shawn and Ralph, the delight and bane of Kimmy's existence, were born in 1980. Unlike Kim, their natural father was Dan who was as proud of them as he was mystified by Kim. Dan loved Kimberly beyond all reason but loved "the red-headed rascals" every bit as much.

Grandma Muriel and Grandpa Brian had led their little tribe to Glenview after knocking around a bit after the war but the three generations were now scattered around this almost-perfect little town. From their home at 2141 Fir Street, the kids could walk across the street to the round community pool in the summer or enjoy ice skating on the snow-covered softball diamonds that were even closer. On the Fourth of July they could walk two blocks to Glenview Avenue and watch a humble but spirited parade. Fireworks could be seen up close a few blocks away but, just across the street, Kim and Company could spread quilts and watch in ease and convenience.

One fun tradition was that, each fall, the swimming pool would be stocked with goldfish for children to net and take home before the pool was drained for the winter. Then too, the Christmas bonfire across the street featured Santa Claus and lots of carmel apples which children ate while dashing about in the dark and crashing into expensive topcoats.

In the winter, there was all too much shoveling of the snow but, in the summertime, one could walk only four blocks for a soft-serve ice cream, a library book, or a Wednesday concert in the park. The park was across the street from the train station which, in the early 1990's was redesigned into a charming replica of a turn of the century destination complete with a turret and all sorts of architectural distinctions. Early in their marriage, Kate and Dan, like her parents, would walk to the train station to commute to work in Chicago. Just across from the station was Kim's favorite landmark. It was a fountain with a bear on top of a column that was the village mascot. This icon led to several "hug the bear" celebrations at various times of the year.

Glenview was almost as Irish and Catholic as Dublin but with many fewer pubs. There were, however, a couple of charming places to tipple near the railway station and, after the softball games, the casual athletes would gather on the porch of one of them to relax before heading home to prepare for the next day's session at work or school.

figure 2:
TRAIN STATION
Glenview, IL

IX: 1991

Kimberly Attends Carmel Catholic H.S.

~

This school is located in in Mundelein, IL and run by the priests and brothers of the Order of Carmelites and Sisters of Charity. There is a uniform dress code and 20 hours of participation in the Christian Service Program per semester are required.

When Kim transitioned from OLPH to Carmel, her mother treated her to do-over at the hairdresser's with the result that her little girl braids were gone and replaced with awesome bangs and floppy hair. Her glossy black hair had the glow and sheen that only youth can impart. As Kate was fond of saying, "Any young woman, if she is clean and cultured, is beautiful. And," Kate would hastily add, "She must have good posture."

So, Kim stood up straight, minded her manners, and with her new hair and obviously budding figure, made quite an impression at her new school. She still maintained and expanded upon her collection of holy cards but, thanks to the internet, was now able to add antique, unique, or exceptional samples of this genre. She also took up an omnivorous interest in the crusades and especially the Knights Templar.

The "Kimster," as she was fondly called by her friends and acquaintances, of whom there were many, tended to be a trend-setter and soon a large number of the CCHS students were wearing white tee-shirts with homemade red Templar crosses underneath their rigidly-regulated school uniforms.

As is the way of adolescents, friendly rivals, and some not quite so friendly, countered by establishing, "The Most Venerable Order of the Hospital of Saint John of Jerusalem" and wearing "Maltese crosses" which consisted of four vee-shaped arms having a total of eight points. Not wishing to argue a distinction without a difference, Kim did not mention that their traditional competitors, the Templars, or "Poor Knights of the Temple of Jerusalem" often wore the same cross as the "Knights Hospitaller." Any sort of cross, as long as it was red to symbolize martyrdom, was worn by either group. In any event, both orders were quite active during the crusades and evolved in interesting ways. The Templars became quite wealthy but their wealth and power eventually led them to fall into disfavor with the Pope and with Philip the Fair who sent out secret orders to arrest all Templars on the same day, Friday, October 13, 1307. Did you ever wonder why Friday the 13th was considered unlucky? Wonder no more.

The priests, brothers, and nuns were bemused by all of this interest in ancient holy orders of warriors but assumed that is was a benign influence and that it gave their charges something to think about other than their hormones.

The Altar Society's annual covered dish supper and St. Patrick's Day dance was a very big deal and, while the women were out shuffling tables around, they left Kim and her little flock of friends in charge of the kitchen. The altar boys, a gang of hooligans to Kimberly's mind, had planned a raid for weeks. They did not realize it but the whole show was intended to make the girls notice them. In any event, while Kim and the others were costuming for the Irish step dancing show, the guys made off with every bowl, plate, and tub of food.

Kim was the first to get back to the kitchen and after taking one look, walked out the back door and then back in. There was then plenty for everyone when it came time to feed the guests and the boys still had a rented van full of food. Someone started a rumor about fishes and loaves but no one could think of who, why, and how.

X: 1991

The Crusades and the Knights Templar

The Crusades began around 1095 when Pope Urban II urged Christians in western Europe to retake Jerusalem. There had been many horror stories about how evilly Christians were being treated in Jerusalem and the rhetoric probably had little resemblance to reality. But the Holy Land was far off and pilgrims were promised loot, adventure, and salvation which had a great appeal in lands where not much was happening except poverty and boredom. Then too, going on this pilgrimage guaranteed salvation and forgiveness of all sins, past, present, and those committed in the future.

While a formidable army of well-equipped and responsible knights was being formed, a rabble rouser called Peter the Hermit gathered a large band of enthusiastic poor folk and set out, willy nilly, ahead of the main army. Peter and his enthusiasts managed to get past Constantinople, just barely, but were wiped out soon thereafter.

In August 1096, Crusaders from several regions set off and, after months, reached Constantinople where Emperor Alexis demanded that they swear fealty to him and turn over to him all lands captured, etc., etc. He was, after, all and in his own mind, the ruler of the Holy Eastern Empire and the interlopers owed him his due. These machinations, and many others which followed, gave rise to the term Byzantine schemes, and similar phrases implying something altogether too cunning and tricky. In any event, most leaders simply took their leave without giving Alexis his due.

The European Knights, wearing what must have felt like tons of armor, carrying large and heavy swords, and mounted on great war horses called destriers were the main battle tanks of their day. Everyone who knows the famous Budweiser clydesdales can imagine them with heavily armored knights perched atop them. For this reason, they quickly captured Antioch in 1098 and Jerusalem on July 1099. When it fell, the Crusaders murdered men, women, and children, Jews, and Moslems alike and it was reported that, at times, the knights waded ankle deep in blood.

The attitude of many Crusaders was then, been there, did that, got the tee shirt, and it is time to go home. Those that remained formed the Crusader states of Jerusalem, Edessa, Antioch, and Tripoli. In 1118, Hugues de Payens and eight other knights bound themselves, to a perpetual vow in the presence of the Patriarch of Jerusalem, to defend the Christian kingdom. Baldwin II, King of Jerusalem accepted them and lodged them in his palace near the temple giving them the name, "Poor Knights of the Temple." Around 1023, the Knights Hospitaller were founded whose mission was to care for poor, sick, or injured pilgrims.

Around 1030, the Muslims began their own holy war and captured Edessa. This led to the second crusade in 1147 and the Muslim city of Damascus was attacked by a force of 50,000 Crusaders but the Crusaders were eventually defeated.

In 1156, the Templars built the mighty Castle Safed and several other fortresses. When the tide turned against the second Crusade in 1264, about 90 Templars died at Safed. The third Crusade, designed to take Egypt, ended up with the Holy Army all-but destroyed but the famous Richard the Lionhearted of England triumphed by winning, at the treaty table, what was not gained by warfare. Saladin signed a treaty that gave the Crusaders the Kingdom of Jerusalem...but not the city itself.

In 1198, the fourth Crusade got only as far as Constantinople with the result that the city was sacked and Byzantine Emperor Alexus III was strangled and the city was looted.

By the 13th century, the whole Crusade business had devolved into a hunt for French heretics and pagans in Transylvania. (What, no werewolves or vampires?) But, Frederick II, called the Holy Roman Emperor, got the Crusades thing going again in1229, but in a weird way. He dithered to and fro about setting off on a Crusade until Pope Gregory IX excommunicated him for failing to take to the road on the Sixth Crusade. Fred did, by proxy, marry Yolande of Jerusalem, heiress to the Kingdom but Freddie's new father-in-law was disposed. In 1228, Fredrick finally sailed to Acre but the administration and Holy Orders (knights, and such) gave him no help at all. He did, however manage to sign a treaty with the Ayyubid Sultan Al-Kamil that returned, to Christian rule, Jerusalem, Nazareth, Bethlehem, and a small costal strip. But the Muslims specifically retained control of the Dome of the Rock and Al-Aqsa Mosque. Many Crusaders on the scene rejected this treaty as a political ploy and, after much squabbling with knights, the Pope, and everyone else in the messy political arena that was ironically called a "Holy Land, " Fredrick went back to Germany where he had pressing business required to retain his home base.

In 1291, The Egyptian Mamulk dynasty retook Acre, the last stronghold of the Crusaders, and virtually all Europeans were driven out of Palestine and Syria.

The Templars remained a force for many years after the Crusades. They had a great deal of influence and, perhaps more importantly, fortress castles, throughout Europe. One main source of their wealth was that they acted as sort of an American Express because pilgrims could give a Templar in Europe their gold and treasure and redeem similar treasure from another Templar when they arrived at the far-distant end of their pilgrimage. This protected them from those pesky bandits and other enemies. The Templars collected fees for these transactions. Then too, these mighty warriors amassed significant loot and plunder from their own victories.

Their property was exempted from all taxes and even church tithes. This did not sit well with the clergy. The Templars were initially the darlings of Popes and the nobility but their wealth and power eventually caused them to earn powerful enemies. In France, they had eleven bailiwicks divided into over forty-two commanderies. Their eventual downfall had no single cause but Philip IV of France was deeply in debt to the Templars and built upon their secret initiation rites a complicated and unbelievable set of charges that no one would have believed un-less it were convenient to do so. And so, on unlucky Friday the thirteenth in October of 1307, the far flung bands of Templars were all arrested at the same time. Torture was a quick way to get "confes-sions" to all sorts of things, and many Templars were burned at the stake. The lack of guilt was no barrier to these executions and the land grab that followed was quite profitable to those who brought false charges. Even though many convictions were later overturned, the Pope disbanded the order in 1312 and nothing is left of the huge wealth of the Templars except legends of hidden treasure and people willing to seek it. The Freemasons also main-tain ties to the Templars of yore with various levels of association. For this reason, the future Kimberly Missions steered away from too-close imitations but no one could claim ownership of a red cross and they continued to use it as their symbol. As far as the "knight" designation, the Kiministas consid-ered themselves to be modern knights. The term "knights of the people' was their official title but "Shining Knights" found favor and they were stuck with it. Freemasons were not intimidated or jealous and felt no need to sue anybody.

XI: 1991

A Fiend Wants Kimmy

~

Satan had wound Gloria up and aimed her at Kim but the other arrow in his quiver was a handsome young custodian that the Devil had encouraged to seek out pornography involving school girls, of which he was surrounded.

Kim was willing to have pajama parties with Gloria but she begged off every time her friend suggested that they practice kissing so that they would be good at it when the boys tried it. Little did she know that Glory had plenty of experience kissing a certain friendly teacher and had even managed a few "frienchies" with the young and "hunky" (Gloria's term) custodian. She was happy to gossip about Kimmie with Clete and got a certain tingle out of speculating whether Kim would be fun to tickle until she "got off."

But Clete's interests were not on the all-too willing Gloria but on Kimberly. Satan had given him his marching orders even if he did not know it and Kim was his target. So he watched when and how she went and where, looking for an opportunity to get her alone and vulnerable.

After her parents took off for the movies, Kim's sleepover guest again wanted to talk about kissing and making out but Kimmie tried to lead her into more wholesome territory. "Tell me Glory, what do you know about angels?"

"Well, after the third grade, the nuns didn't talk much about angels but gave equal time to history, multiplication, pagan babies, and animal husbandry."

"Pagan babies?" Asked Kim, "What's with that?"

"They seemed to be an excuse to relieve us of a part of our lunch money to support missions in far off lands. Most classes would adopt a "pagan baby" in Borneo, Zimbabwe, or some other unknown place. My class really got into it and named our pagan baby, Leroy. But, I preferred to save my change for an Eskimo Pie."

"I don't know about your Leroy Gloria but dont'cha think that we should all love the needy and help them whenever we can? We should try to be some kind of human guardian angels to those that we can help."

"What do you know about angels, Kim?"

"Our nun was really into them. She said that the Egyptian hawk-god, Horus, had wings but the angels in the Bible were pretty commonplace and looked just like everyone else. The three angels that Abraham asked to spare Sodom, the angel by Christ's tomb, and the angel that was seen in the fire with Shadrach, Mesach, and Abednego were described only as men whose presence could not be accounted for. And Jacob wrestled all night with an angel but did not seem to know what he had his hands on. The most detailed description of angels was by Ezekiel who described cherubim as "wheels.""

"How would we recognize an angel Kim?"

"We were taught that, in the 6th century, Pope Gregory the Great invited 12 men to dinner but 13 showed up and they later decided that he was an angel. In other words, we could walk by an angel on the street but would never know it."

Gloria brought out some "dirty pictures" that she tried to interest Kim in but Kimmie talked her into studying Kim's collection of holy cards depicting the lives of saints and martyrs. Some were rare, and some quite beautiful and Gloria soon became engrossed in something wholesome for a change.

Kim good-naturedly accepted what she thought of as Gloria's quirky interests and Gloria loved The Kimster so they remained BFF. No harm, no foul.

When Gloria told Clete that Kim had foolishly decided to go off with the youth group on a late night vigil at the church, he saw an opportunity. He knew that the priest had a habit of nodding off whenever he passed his regular bedtime and Clete was well aware that the young sinners, as he called them, sometimes snuck off in pairs for a little innocent fondling that was, to their inexperienced minds, rip-roaring sex.

From the supply closet in the girl's restroom, Clete patiently waited for Kim to have a need to visit. He inspected many others and was well primed by the time that a yawning Kimberly showed up about 3 in the morning.

As she emerged from the stall, he dropped a bag over her head and gave her a slap that stunned her while he slid a set of zip-ties around her wrists. Upending her, he zip-tied her ankles and noticed that she had a nice chaste set of pink panties.

Time for that later, he thought. He hauled her out a convenient service door and dumped her in the back of his panel truck. As he roared away, he chortled with glee at having achieved something that he had dreamed about for months.

Somewhere "below" Satan was cheering. Gloria had failed but good buddy Clete was nearing the goal-line.

"God Dammit!" yelled Inspector Patrick Garcia! "Everyone get in here!"

The detectives knew that something really bad had happened if Paddy was cussing. He was the original stone-face and nothing bothered him.

"Well, boys and girls, we have a situation! Some Catholic teenager has gone missing from a Holy Vigil or whatever. The priest is about to spit holy water out of his ears and her parents are both "PILLARS OF THE COMMUNITY! Got that? Priests and pillars!"

" Penny and Yolanda, go interview the priest! Yes, CCHS! Where else?"

"Gregorio and Freeman, round up the kids! See if anyone saw anything."

"Buster, you are the only one left. Go talk to the parents. Be tactful!"

When she heard what had happened, Gloria thought briefly of Clete but, there he was, pushing the big broom just as he always did. Why would anyone want Kimmie? Thinking about exactly why gave her a flush. She had let such a fantasy give her many hours of forbidden thoughts and pleasure but Kimmie was her friend and she hoped, as she knew that it was unlikely, that Kim was safe and just, somehow, misplaced.

When Officer Gregorio got around to Gloria, she was of no help and had no information that she was willing to share. Clete's interest in schoolgirls might have reflected upon her and she was her own best friend, first and foremost. Kimmie was in no danger from Clete. She was too prudish for him, unlike some other students who had needs! And so, an opportunity for Kimberly's quick release was squandered.

Clete had stashed his captive in the basement dungeon he had lovingly prepared over the last year. The basement of a long-dead aunt was completely off the radar and not likely to be discovered. But now that he had her, Clete was afraid to fulfill the fantasies what had tormented and delighted him. He locked her up with a couple of happy meals and took off. She had water from a sink, a mattress on the floor, a bathroom, and light from a dusty bulb. Clete was satisfied that she would keep for a while. Of course, he would have to kill her but he must make thorough use of her first. Otherwise, the whole thing would have been a terrible waste.

On the way back to Glenview, he searched out and captured a dozen stray dogs and a few unlucky pets and left them in his van while he did his daily rounds at CCHS. When got around to playing the benefactor and rescuer of lost critters, he not only earned the praise of the local Animal Protection Society but had acquired enough "trace" in the form of cast off hair, blood from dogfights and waste from unhousebroken dogs to confound any future criminologist. Human hair from many transfers by owners and their children made the whole van even more impossible for any criminologist to process.

After a couple of days of, "Should I?, Dare I ?, and Must I?" Gloria retreated to her room and just cried. When she looked for a Kleenex in her pocket, she pulled out a crumpled holy card. Also called prayer cards, they usually had a picture of a saint or religious scene one one side and a prayer or memoriam for a baptism, confirmation, funeral, or such on the reverse. What she found was St. Joan of Arc. This unlikely young girl was the daughter of French peasants who heard the voices of Saints Michael,

Catherine, and Margaret telling her to go to the King of France and help him to reconquer the kingdom held by England. After many fortuitous events, she managed to be given a small army and sent off to raise the siege of Orleans. They probably did this just to get rid of this troublesome waif but, much to the surprise of everyone except Joan, she succeeded in May, 1429.

After many other miraculous victories, Joan entered Rheims at the side of Charles where he was crowned. Hubris led her to attempt one battle too many and, at the battle of Compiegne, she was captured by the Burgundians and sold to the English.

Neither the ungrateful wretch, King Charles, not the jealous French came to her aid and she was burned at the stake as a heretic, sorceress, and adulteress. The last, and most unlikely, charge, probably had its source in the way she was treated in captivity. Thirty years later, she was exonerated and, in 1920, she was made a saint.

Gloria had been indoctrinated in the mythic activities of the Crusading Knights by Kim and, coupled with the inspiration of St. Joan, she picked up the phone and called 911. Soon she was surrounded by cops and Patrick Garcia, in particular, who wrung from her enough information to sic their not inconsiderable resources on the trail of Clete whatshisname.

Meanwhile, far, far, away, Kim was huddled in the corner of her basement cell but she could hear Clete singing bawdy ditties as he hammered, and sawed, and drilled, and bolted. His "sex machine" was nearly finished. He intended to strap her here and there and do this and that to her before turning her over and forcing her to do everything else that he could think of. And, with Lucifer as his unconscious guide, he could think of a lot. Clete finished and turned toward the dungeon shaking, not with fear, but with uncontrollable anticipation. He picked up a length of chain, grabbed the key to Kim's door and...

...and the room exploded with the radiance of the sun and a very angry angel pointing a flaming sword at Clete who, at that moment could have used a diaper to catch what diapers usually capture. "Spawn of Satan! Creature of Lucifer! Ploy of Beelzebub! Prepare for Hell!"

Clete believed it! He could not deny all that was made known to him in the instant before he was consumed in a flame that burned nothing but this worthless thing who had willingly sold his soul.

The infernal machine was also burnt into un-identifiable scraps so when the police armada screeched to a stop in front of the farmhouse, there was nothing to do but to unlock the door and re-lease a mildly traumatized but fortunately unaware little girl. Patrick never revealed where the timely tip had come from and Clete was never again seen by mortal man.

A few blocks away, a funny little man in a three-piece brown suit and wearing a bowler hat strolled down the road. He is puffing a fat cigar, that should smell horrible but whose smoke reminds passersby of the incense that permeated the cathedral at their last High Roman mass.

XII: 1995

Kimberly Goes to College

~

After Kim had settled into her little dorm room, she was surprised to receive a formal invitation to spend the weekend at a "gathering of family" at a nearby and very posh inn. The invitation said, "pack comfortable clothes."

She was the first to arrive and again surprised to find that it was a magnificent suite with four large bedrooms on each of the four sides.

"Kim, dear," Said her mother when she arrived, "We are here to tell you what you need to know as you leave home and face life alone."

"Everyone is here but where are my brothers Shawn and Ralph?"

"Surprisingly, they are not part of the mystery that we are here to reveal. They are part of our family and we all love them gobs and heaps but they would be disadvantaged in their growing up to know what we need to talk about tonight. Let Granny Muriel start."

"Kimmie, I want to tell you about evil and how flowers can grow out of the wreckage of one's life. You have read my "Dachau Devotionals" so you know some of what I experienced but the story does not begin there. My father, Israel Cohen, made a thorough study of our ancestry and he claimed that he could trace, but unfortunately not prove, our ancestry back to King David. Jesus was descended from David and we obviously were not descended from Him but, somewhere along the line, we were cousins or somewhere along the family tree. Perhaps Mary had a brother, or uncle, or some near-miss on the family but obviously Joseph is not a candidate because he was not the father of Jesus and you ARE, in some way, related to Jesus. "

Kate added, "Not to get ahead of the story but the Angel told me that you were the sister of Jesus, meaning you had the same father.

"What!" said Kim.

"We will get to that later. Just let Mother Muriel continue."

"After that bombshell, she better get to the point quickly." muttered Kim who was beginning to feel very discomforted with the direction this evening was taking.

Brian said, "After all of the killing in the war, I was happy to pass the time sorting piles of war surplus clothes. Others were in charge of hardware, guns, and tanks and all that, but my main job was to separate the too bloody and torn from the reusable. After months of mindless drudgery, I found that one of the many helpers began to appear on the fringes of my limited attention span. More and more, I was drawn to this beautiful waif with the large sad eyes and very female body that the shapeless and dusty dresses could not conceal."

Grannie Muriel interrupted, "I did manage to put a few pounds back on with the free lunch of the messy mess hall. The food was pretty basic but, when so many were starving and would sell their body for a pork chop, I felt blessed to have one meal a day. I also had my eye on that handsome GI who never seemed to notice me."

"Anyway, after some circling around, we came together with a crash of love and passion that melted two people into one. She was a passionate little thing and I was young and capable. I felt inadequate to match her fierce love for me but decided that, if she loved me that hard, I could grow to love her just as much."

Clapping his hands together, Grandpa Brian says, "Well Kim, we didn't need that digression but we are here to unload upon you the family secrets and the meaning of life, both washed and unwashed. Now, let Your mother have a go."

"Kim. Prepare yourself for a story beyond imagining or belief. I know you will never forget the circumstances of your release from the frightful fiend that kidnapped you. You said an angel got rid of your kidnapper but we told you that it was all an hallucination caused by drugs you were given."

"But, Mom! I kept dreaming a fuzzy dream about this monstrous angel that slammed a flaming sword into my captor and yelled that he was being sent straight to Hell."

"Kim dear, it was true. You did not dream it. There are guardian angels and your remarkable streak of luck was not luck but the work of an angel that is always with you. He appeared to me even before you were born and has been with us both ever since."

"Wait Kim! There is more. You say the Rosary and I know you know the Joyful Mysteries very well. Please say them for me."

Kim said, "The first Joyful Mystery is the Annunciation of Mary. The second is The Visitation of Mary. The third, The Nativity of Our Lord, the fourth, The Presentation of the Baby Jesus at the Temple. And finally, The Finding of the Child Jesus in the Temple. BUT WHAT, DOES THIS HAVE TO DO WITH ME?"

"The Angel Samuel visited me just as Gabriel visited Mary."

"Good God!" cried Kim, "What are you telling me?"

"Meet the Angel Samuel, Kim"

Sammy got up off the la-Z-boy, smiled, and tipped his hat.

"You don't look much like an angel to me!" Kim said.

Sammy winked mischievously and said, "Glad to oblige. Hold on to your hat kiddo."

And, with that, he went into full-angel mode: white wings, shining gleaming gold breastplate, white kilt and lace-up sandals. Rather than a dough-faced old man with a five o'clock shadow, this countenance was literally divine.

"So that is what beatific looks like." said the always irreverent Kim. "I kinda like the golden locks too. Good makeover, Unka Samuel. Glad ta meet-cha. And now I am just babbling." Said Kim with her usual capability for self-analysis.

"Poof! Here I am again. Good old Uncle Sammy. Are you more comfortable with this image?"

"Yes, Thank you. I guess I needed to know that but, if you are an angel, a messenger, what is your message for ME?"

"Just this, well... not just, ...but to begin with, you are indeed the child of God, sister of Jesus and you have come to fight in the ultimate battle. The Armageddon is almost upon us and you will have a large role in the outcome. So go back to school tomorrow and let what will be, be. You will know what to do when you need to do it. The Grace of God will never let you go beyond where you need to be. And, finally, be not be afraid of your mighty powers. Your Brother could raise the dead, cure the lepers, and, yet he let himself die on the cross. Be comforted that you will not be martyred but will live long and prosper."

The ever practical Dan nodded toward Muriel and Brian sitting in shock in the corner and said, "We better give Granny and Gramps something to drink and answer their questions. They are as much in shock as Kimmie would be if she were not the handmaiden of God. Oh, wait! Kate is the handmaiden. Who would have thunk it? My old wife the virgin mother of God, or is it Goddess?...must be Goddess! Congratulations Kimmie."

As intended, Dan's little interlude restored a semblance of calm and Sammy helped by answering everyone's questions with honesty and, when necessary, digression.

Dan said, "Kimmie, Joseph was convinced by an angel that the virgin Mary was a pure and worthy wife and Samuel did the same for me. Joseph did not have a knowledge of biological sciences so Sammy had a harder time convincing me but, when God sends his messenger, no one remains unconvinced. All that is left is the explaining why. I was given to know some things about you and the world to come that I could not speak of even should I have the desire, which I do. I love you just as if you were my own flesh but I am also in awe of what you are. I can tell you that you have come to save the world...again!"

Dan continued, "Kim, I can give you a hint. I think. If Armageddon is to be the battle between good and evil, does it not follow that the returning child of God would be a warrior? ...And, might be a girl? You always admired Joan of Arc and the Templars. Yes, I see a warrior spirit in you."

"If, after 2,000 years, the message of peace and love has not protected the innocent from evildoers; might not God decide to try a different direction? More Old Testament, so to speak. Let's talk about Sampson and those he slew with the jawbone of an ass. Or Joshua at the battle of Jericho when the walls came tumbling down. Or, your distant relative, David and what happened to Goliath."

And so they talked a bit about the more vengeful God of the Old Testament and those he chose to mete out justice to transgressors. Everyone had someone or some battle to contribute but Sammy's contributions were usually unknown to all but him.

Kim got up the morning after the family gathering, had a quiet breakfast with one and all, and headed back to Liberty University. She had her room on campus and the usual belongings of a freshman student. And so, she passed her first two years in mundane study and social activities. Her junior year was to prove more challenging.

When Kim decided to become a history major, she was asked to face a panel from the American History Department and tell them a little something that she had learned about American history. Ever poised, she began with an interesting story:

"When the Pilgrims came to America, they nearly starved until an Indian showed up speaking English. They were stunned to find a savage from a place never visited by "white men" who spoke their language. How could that be? It was if a little green man from outer space showed up in the Ozarks speaking fluent English."

"Well, Squanto showed the starving Pilgrims how to plant dead fish with each corn seed to fertilize the soil. A typical Indian garden consisted of the "three sisters." That is, corn, beans to grow up the corn stalk, and squash to grow on the ground under it. The Pilgrims learned and survived."

"Wait, Miss Ryan! How did the Native American learn English?" Professor Hillbert continued, "The Pilgrims were from an advanced civilization compared to the local "savages" but were not hacking it where they were. Squanto arrived on the scene like the cartoon Mighty Mouse who used to say, "Hooray! Here I am to save the day!"

"Who?" Said Kim.

"Excuse me. It seems that you are not as familiar with movie history as I am. How did this Indian learn to speak English?"

"Well, it seems that he was kidnapped around 1614 by early explorers of the Americas or fishermen and taken to Spain where he was sold as a slave. By luck and pluck he made his way to London where he made himself useful to a nobleman and earned passage back to the land from whence he came. When he reached the the Americas at about the spot where his tribe had lived, he found that they had all died of smallpox or some other imported disease. Alone and lonely, he joined another band of Native Americans and eventually contacted the settlers in Plymouth where he helped them survive by teaching them the tricks I described earlier and by helping them to learn many other useful survival skills."

Kim concluded, "Well, can I get into your department?

And, she was welcomed with enthusiasm by all members of the panel. Old Hillbert even invited her to tea the following afternoon.

XIII: 1997

The Fight for Gloria's Soul

~

When Kim was a junior, about age 22, Gloria transferred to LibU and asked to become Kim's roommate. They were, after all BFF, and not even the passage of time had dulled Kim's affection for her old partner in innocent skulduggery. If Gloria had her way, the skulduggery would have been less innocent but "The Kimster", as "Glory" still called her, was a pretty good influence even to one with a devil on her shoulder whispering in her ear.

Kim was a little bit shocked and a lot curious about Glory's appearance. If it had been in her vocabulary, she would have characterized her friend as looking a little slutty and a lot hot. Gloria still wanted to play "kissy-face" but Kim restricted her to sisterly pecks on the cheek as a good-night tradition. Gloria slept in the nude and constantly urged Kim to get rid of her "granny pajammies" but Kim would have none of it. No amount of hinting or even pleading would talk Gloria out of prancing around "starkers" as she called it and lecturing on the health and emotional benefits of nudity.

Kim either had to put up with it or toss her room-mate out on her pretty little ear. Glory distracted Kim from her studies with wild tales of wanton adventures that Glory seemed to feel pretty proud of. The Devil tempted Jesus in the desert but he tempted Kim in her dorm room. When Kim dared to look closely, she noticed a green tattoo of a grinning goat skull high up on Gloria's inner thigh. Kim had been shamed into trying a few margaritas that Gloria had laced with Rohypnol and was willing to join in a couple's shower followed by a vigorous toweling off. As she gave herself into a warm embrace and was being lowered into the bed, that goat tattoo screamed up from the depths of her libido. "Lucifer!" She yelled. "Satan! Beelzebub! Go away! and you too Gloria! The goat tattoo shows that you have been marked by Satan!" Then, with authority, Kimberly called, "Sammy! Samuel! Come here! I need you now!"

With the crack of thunder and lightning, Samuel appeared in full drag. "You called, Kim? How may I serve you?"

If Gloria were a cartoon character, her eyes would have popped out of her head on springs but she was not so she only stared goggle-eyed at the glowing apparition that stood before her, golden breastplate, spread wings, and the whole sheebang.

"Samuel, my friend has had a little too much Devil worship. Envelop her in your arms to remove her sins and reverse her evil habits."

"Kimberly, no one or no being has ever asked this of me. Are you sure...?"

"Did not Jesus drive evil spirits into swine and then run them into the sea? Surely you can handle one young woman!"

"Ok-dokey, Kim. You are the boss!"

Gloria recovered her natural chutzpah long enough to shout, "You? Kim? The boss of this, this... thing?"

Samuel folded his arms and wings around Gloria who felt peace and contentment like she had never felt or believed possible. Now, this was living! "I want more of it!," she screamed.

Kim smiled and said, "Well Gloria, I guess that is what the Baptists would call being born again. How do you like it so far? And, Samuel please go back to Sammy"

POP! ...and a funny little man in a derby hat sat smoking his sweet smelling cigar in the one chair of their dorm room.

"Now what?" Gloria said, "Where did your angel go and who is this guy? Men are not allowed in the women's residence hall."

"You saw with your own eyes that he is no man. Sammy is Samuel, only more informally dressed. Does, "Go and sin no more?" Sound familiar? Well, I say it to you. We can still be friends, only real friends without the cloak of Satan concealing your better nature. We should all try to love those who have lost their way and try to redirect them to a better path"

And so, Gloria did find the better way. She graduated with honors, became a social worker, and ended up with a Baptist minister for a husband. She had been "born-again" twice but she was the first to truly recognize the sanctity of "The Kimster." When Kim later officially became Saint Kimberly, Gloria sent an engraved congratulations note and an invitation to bring Sammy and come visit her and her children.

Gloria had become more Cleaver than June, wearing pearls with her aprons, of which she had a vast collection. Few remembered "the Beaver" who reigned on TV from 1957 to 1963 so Gloria's son Theodore, called Teddy, was assumed to be named after a famous President. Behind her back, certain catty neighbors referred to this perfect mother as a "Stepford Wife." Gloria was not insulted but reveled in the irony.

XIV: 1999

Escape to a Convent

~

Kim graduated from LU with a degree in History with emphasis on the eras covered by the New Testament, the several crusades, and the colonization of America and its liberation. After the emotional stress of her senior year, she decided to enter a convent for a period of hard work and spiritual reflection. She felt a need for renewal and believed that this would be a good interlude before what she instinctually knew was just over the hill, so to speak.

Unknowingly, she was guided by a higher power to the Convent of the Sisters of the Holy Mount, casually and irrelevantly called "The Mountaineers." This group had been founded around 1128 when the Knights Templars led by Hugues de Payens assisted at the Council of Troyes. St. Bernard was a leader at this meeting and the Knights adopted the rule of St. Benedict and the white habit of the Cistercians to which they added a red cross. As described earlier, these warrior monks soon became wealthy and a force to be reckoned with in medieval Europe.

The Sisters of the Holy Mount, spiritual kin of the Templars and, in the early years, often more than platonic associates, wore habits similar to those of the templars excepting for the addition of a white wimple covering the hair and neck. In those days, chastity was, even among Popes who often had children, more optional among the religious than today.

When she entered the convent, Uncle Ben showed up to donate a significant number of Templar Doves and began building a large roost for them. Not one to indulge in half measures, when Ben finished, the resulting rookery resembled a medieval fortress similar those inhabited by the knights of yore. The Mother Superior was pleased by the linking of their history with these beautiful doves and, ever practical, also looked forward to an expansion of their limited menu.

While Kim was learning about the cloistered life, her brothers were beginning their higher education. Ralph was in seminary and determined to become a priest. Shawn was at MIT and determined to become a millionaire by inventing stuff that only one as brilliant as he could devise. Shawn may not have been modest but he had an accurate evaluation of his capabilities.

After several months of discipline and prayer, Kim became more comfortable with her surroundings and developed many friends among the novitiates. One special pal was Sister Baldwin who seemed to know everything about everything that went on in the vast establishment that they inhabited.

One day, Kim asked Baldy, as they called her for no good reason, "What is with that little building set aside from the rest of the facilities?"

"Oh, That is the penitent's cloister. Nuns who have need of special spiritual succor live there supervised by the most reverent among us who can provide guidance in their journey back from the bad habits (no pun intended) that they have fallen into."

"Do you know any of them?" Kim asked.

"Well, don't repeat this but I have heard that there is a certain Sister Fortunate, or some name like that, who was sent here after being found to have led astray some of her students. The principal

of the school caught her in the confessional per-
forming an extremely sinful oral act upon a student
named Gillian? no!, Grace?, no!…it was Gloria!"

"Anyway, it seems that this teacher had made a
habit of "spanking" the boys and girls after slowly
rubbing their bottoms until she found "just the
right spot" and then giving them a sudden slap. A
few of the students seemed to get off on this and
found excuses to be "disciplined." No one knows,
but I bet that she created more than a few masoch-
ists and a sadist or two as these kids grew up. In
any event, she has been sent here to consider the
error of her ways but I hear that she is such a hard
case that they are considering summoning a priest
to perform the rite of exorcism."

"Wow, Baldy, that is pretty sad, both for this
failed nun and the children that she led astray"

As the girls went back to their chores, Kim was
thinking that this explained a lot about how her
childhood friend became what she became and
why her own innocent and inexperienced self had
felt uneasy and "creepy" whenever this teacher was
around.

After a year of submission and discipline, Kim
was given the grace to discern that she was ready to
become what she was sent to be. She loved the peace

and serenity that the morning mass brought but she began to discern that the visiting priest, Father Medici, supposedly from Tuscany, was a little "off." In what way, she could not say but she smelled a rat, so to speak, in those vestments. There were several visiting priests cycling through the convent but this one was not like all the others. For one thing, his behavior in the confessional box suggested that he wanted to lead the penitent to deal with sins of their past lives in more detail than omissions and sins of the present day.

After questioning several of the younger and more recent entries into the convent, Kim determined that they were being more or less forced into revealing the more tawdry episodes of their earlier years in considerable detail. A few even felt that they were being offered subtle opportunities to meet with the priest outside of the confessional box but no one had dared to even consider that they were being offered what they thought they were being offered.

Kim decided to take matters into her own strong but tiny hands and so, late one evening, she entered the confessional when she knew Father Medici was hearing confessions. She led him on with increasingly suggestive revelations and eventually agreed to meet him in the stables after mass. When he showed up, Kim said, "Father, get down on your knees. I am going to show something that I think that you will like."

"Goodie, goodie" he said, nearly drooling as he imagined many scenarios but not the one that Kim had in mind.

Kim had summoned her friend Sammy earlier and he appeared when beckoned.

"Behold! The Angel Samuel!" Kim shouted as the fiery apparition appeared in the dark stable. "Run away false priest! Far, Far away and remove your priestly disguise. Never again appear to others as a priest or this angel will appear and be less merciful than he is today!"

After a very quick departure in wet trousers, the ex-Father Medici was never seen again, anywhere, by anyone.

Her mother and Grammy Muriel had given her the knowledge to know her heritage and the Holy Spirit made her known to herself. She decided to give herself another test that came in the form of the poor Sister Fortuna who had resisted exorcism, prayer, and intensive counseling with both psychoanalytic and religious intentions. Kim got up off her knees in the chapel one morning and boldly walked over to the segregated housing where her target resided.

When she opened the door to Fortuna's quarters, the wretch cried out, "You! Have you come, like the others, to save my soul? Well it won't work! Better than you have tried! And failed!"

"I see Satan in you Sister." Kim said in a quiet voice. "I have not come to save you but to give you back to God."

Fortuna was dumbstruck as Kim folded her into a loving embrace and said nothing. No words, no exhortations, just loving acceptance that flowed from Kim to what was left of the woeful Molly who had been led astray.

"Molly, become that little girl who you were before Satan recruited you to snare me. You did not snare me but I have snared you and set you free from your slavery. The unknowing recruit into the forces of darkness is given her discharge papers. Take the name Sister Mary Magdalene after the one who was cured of seven devils and became the friend of Jesus. Just as she was the first to know that he had risen, you are the first to know that his sister has come."

"You! Oh, my God!" The new Sister MM prostrated herself and cried out, "Forgive me Kimberly. I was …."

"You know that are forgiven. Now get up and go ask the Mother Superior of this order to enroll you as a novice under your new name. Do not tell her what has happened here but keep it in your heart. Just know that you will do good works and redeem yourself in your own eyes. God does not need proof of what you will accomplish. He already knows."

"By the way, Sister MM, it will comfort you to know that Gloria has been salvaged from the wreckage you caused and has turned her life around."

"Thank you. It does help to know that. I have plenty of other stuff to atone for."

XV: 2001

Leaving the Convent

~

When the passenger jets hit the World Trade Centers, Kim knew that her interlude was over. It was time to leave the quiet cloisters and the sweet murmuring in the chapel and take up the cross and gauntlet. The war was beginning. President Bush was quite capable of handling the physical shock and awe but the Holy War that lay underneath the coming of Ahmadinejad was just beginning. He, and others, dreamed of a world-wide Caliphate extending to the entire Muslim faithful and ruled by sharia (Islamic law). Kim's response to the situation was, "Not on my watch, Buster!"

Kim recalled Edmund Burke's announcement that, "The only thing necessary for the triumph of evil is for good men to do nothing." And, women, Kim added to herself.

Ahmadinejad sometimes seemed to fancy himself the "12th Imam" who will usher in the day of judgment that will result in a world-wide Caliphate by obliterating Israel. To him, a nuclear war would be "a good start." It is not likely that he is the 12th Imam because Shias believe that the 12th Imam (called the Mahdi) was born in the 800's and hidden by God (their God) until the day of judgement.

At age 25, Kim was ready to get on with it and graciously asked the Prioress to dismiss her. When her resignation was regretfully accepted, she borrowed the convent's only phone to ask her mother to come pick her up and was told that she would arrive late the next day. She then decided to spend the time waiting until she could be picked up in visiting the physically sick in the convent clinic. Due to declining volunteers to the monastic life, the age range of the sisters trended toward the old. With that territory came illness and various aches and pains.

Sister Veronica was a favorite of everyone in the house and admired for the fortitude she displayed coping with end-stage cancer of practically every organ of her body. She greeted Kim with a wan smile and gratefully accepted the offer to pray the Rosary. Since it was Thursday, they included the five Luminous Mysteries; The Baptism of Christ in the Jordan, The Wedding Feast at Cana. The Proclamation of the Kingdom, The Transfiguration, and The Institution of the Eucharist.

They concluded, as always, "O GOD, whose only begotten Son, by his life, death, and resurrection has purchased for us the rewards of eternal life, grant, we beseech Thee, that meditating upon these mysteries of the most Holy Rosary of the Blessed Virgin Mary, we may imitate what they contain, and obtain what they promise: through the same Christ our Lord. Amen."

Veronica then fell into a painless sleep for the first time in many, many, months. It would not be until Kim was long gone and far away that it become known that the cancer had been wholly eradicated and all other aches and pains gone. Sister V. would go on to live a long and productive life and know, in the fullness of time, that this first of many miracles would be instrumental in discerning the sainthood of Kimberly. When the Pope personally visited to inquire about these events, the convent would gain international attention and the problem of declining membership would be solved by a flood of applicants.

Kimberly knew that her life's work would be to seek out the weak to love and raise up so that they could fulfill their destiny.

Many others of the sick and hurting were visited that day and, without exception, all were relieved of their troubles, whether physical or mental.

The ward was soon emptied and the entire congregation stayed healthy forever after. They attributed their good fortune to prayer, hard work, good food, and divine protection of their order. A few were even even secretly and silently convinced that it was the work of a saint who had come and gone with little fanfare. Later, even the Pope would agree with this suspicion.

As Kim and Kate drove away, the Sisters who had gathered to see her off watched in wonderment as the entire flock of Templar Doves left their roost and circled over the car and then followed for a ways before returning to their home on the grounds of the the convent.

XVI: 2002

Jackpot! the Lottery Funds the Missions

~

Kate was deliriously happy to have her child back but soon came to realize that this was a child no more. She shared her car with an intelligent and poised young woman who seemed to have a lot on her mind. They were probably both remembering the long discussion they had when Kimmie entered college and neither doubted Kim's essential divinity but she did not show any of the outward trappings of a Goddess. But then, neither had her brother, Jesus.

And so they chattered about inconsequential things and were content to merely enjoy the companionship. After many hours of driving, they stopped for gas, Cokes, and a restroom break. When they returned to the car and drove away, Kim waved a small scrap of parer and said, "Guess what,

Ma? I bought a ticket for the PowerLotto. It says that the jackpot is knocking at the door of 500 million. I could do some good with that sort of bonanza."

An hour or so down the road, Kim said, "Mom, I skipped a step about buying the lottery ticket. I ran into Uncle Sammy while you were in the loo. He was eating a corn dog and how he could do that with his ubiquitous cigar stuffed in his cheek, was a sight to see. But I digress. I told him a little of my leaving the convent and he said, "Then you will need to buy a lottery ticket." I was amused and even let him dictate the numbers for me. Anyway, he told me not to tell you that he was in this neck of the woods, as he put it, and I assumed that he had his reasons.

"Kimmie, the man you have always known as Uncle Sammy is more that just the Uncle from somewhere else that drops in for the occasional Thanksgiving of Easter celebration."

"Yes, Mother," Said Kim with just a little bit of what all daughters feel about their clueless mothers, "Remember our talk when I went off to college?"

Her mother would never know how Kim had introduced Gloria to an angel to save her soul. Indeed, she and Samuel were well known to each other in ways that her mother would never be told.

"As a child" Kim said, "I never wondered how he was related and to whom. He was always just the fun, friendly, funny little man who showed up from time to time. I always pretended that he was my secret leprechaun with his bald head accented with a teardrop of red hair over his forehead. I was fascinated that he always wore a brown suit with a vest and that the suits were obviously never the same one because their weight, weave, and style always varied. Then too, he always wore a green necktie but the pattern was always different. I was disappointed when it was not shamrocks but he sported horses, hunting dogs, sailing ships, stripes, and plaids, all without prejudice toward any particular design."

"O.K. Kim. Here is the deal. remember the shocking conversation your Dad and I had with you when you entered college? The angel Samuel who appeared to us with glowing wings, golden armor, and beautiful countenance was, in his more informal, aspect, Sammy."

"Unka Sammy is the Angel Samuel, the annunciator?" And, she managed to say that with a straight face.

"Yep. He says that he feels more at ease in human society in this guise. Haven't you noticed that his cigar never drops ashes on the carpet and always smells faintly like the incense used at high mass?"

"I did notice that it did not stink like all other cigars. And no, I did not discern any angelic action at work when I was little. He was the one that gave me my first holy card and shared my interest in my little collection which grew into a significant hobby. What better way to teach a little girl about her faith and to provide laudable examples to follow? What a clever angel. I guess I had a guardian angel all along just like the stories the nuns liked to tell."

And so it came to pass that the nonprofit "Kimberly Mission Foundation (KMF)" was founded with a piece of paper "fortuitously" (?) picked up at a run-down service station somewhere on the road to Illinois. Clever lawyers structured a nonprofit religious trust to collect the winnings so that the usual tax ripoffs were minimized, but not, and never, eliminated. Even so, a net of 300 million was a darn good start.

Kim lost no time in setting up an organization divided into secular offices (SOs) to protect and increase the principal and religious cadres (RCs) to do humanitarian work. The RCs could veto any incursions by the SOs but not the reverse.

Having foreknowledge of what was to come, Kim had a unpublished agenda which was implied but never stated. All members were gathered by teleconferencing at the beginning of each week and all newcomers were given the original statement of organizing principals that Kim expressed in her first all-hands-on-deck speech. This summarized in the following abbreviated form:

"Welcome one and all. You have joined an informal but serious coeducational monastic order. It is, you will be happy to know, not celibate but, at the same time, not promiscuous. We are all brothers and sisters committed to doing good work. We are also committed to fight the Devil and all of his very real manifestations.

The Knights of The Temple, or Templars, started with nine knights but grew into a strong force for good. That they were less than always holy and true is only to be expected of mere humans. Even after being warned in advance, Simon Peter could not remain faithful until the cock crowed.

But, I digress.

I have long studied and admired the Templars as militant and triumphant forces in support of God and his purposes. We will use them as a model for our organization. We are to do good but, more importantly, to fight evil.

Before he ascended the Mount of Olives on that last night, Jesus said the following as documented in Luke 22:31-32, "And the Lord said, "Simon, Simon! Indeed, Satan has asked for you, that he may sift you as wheat. But I have prayed for you, that your faith shall not fail; and when you have returned to Me, strengthen your brethren."

And again in Luke 22: 36-38, He said to them, "But now, he who has a money bag, let him take it, and likewise, a knapsack; and he who has no sword, let him sell his garment and buy one. For I say to you that this which is written must still be accomplished in Me: 'and he was numbered with the transgressors.' "For the things concerning Me have an end." So they said, "Lord, look here are two swords." And he said to them,"It is enough."

Make no mistake about it. I have knowledge that the end times are coming when the forces of good and evil will physically clash. But first the winnowing will occur as sides are taken. Godliness against Holy, hedonists against serious followers of the Commandments, and those who demand the freedom to rut and abort against those who would protect the innocent unborn. These are only a small sample but endless others are before your eyes if you are willing to see.

The Kimberly Mission Foundation requires a commitment and a willingness to risk all in defense of something greater than yourself. The road is hard and will be long but, live or die, I guarantee that you will find joy.

We will have four ranks of brethren:
the knights, ready to fight with sword and deeds
the sergeants, supporting the knights and hoping to advance to knight
the administrators who are entrusted to keeping the ship afloat
the chaplains who are priests and ministers and attend to the spiritual
needs of us and those we seek to help.

Only the knights will wear the uniform consisting of a tunic with a red cross and a ceremonial sword that is fully functional. The outer garment will be a short brown cape fastened with a round enamel pin with a Templar Dove on a light blue background.

If you are not ready to stand against Armageddon in the future and the blandishments of Satan in the present, we wish you well as you leave to seek other, less challenging, pursuits.

At this point, most new recruits left and those that remained were sufficient unto the task.

The first task, with a budget of 20 million, was the building of what she called the shining temple on a hill. The "shining temple" was constructed of reflective aluminum bricks and assembled in the form of a Templar fortress. Finding a significant hill in the suburbs of Chicago was no easy task but adding many, many cubic yards of rubble and fill to a cornfield outside of Glenview made a sufficiently high point. Full-grown trees, both conifers and deciduous, were brought to the site to fashion a charming forest to surround the property. If Walt could transform a Florida swamp into a Disney Africa, then, with the help of some moonlighting Disney architects and engineers, Kim could create a replica of a Templar fortress. The property was not featured in any recruiting brochure but committed newcomers felt their decision to be validated when they arrived at the place where they were to live and work. To avoid social and physical isolation, a "visitors village" was built at the edge of the forest near a charming babbling brook. The brook and chirping birds were sort of "anamatronic", which is deliberately misspelled to avoid hassles from Disney copyright lawyers.

With the passage of time, the cadre of those advancing to knight status grew and they were sent out with the following.

a staff because they were to walk upon reaching their destination.

a backpack containing:

a Bible, a GPS/satphone, a copy of the U.S. Constitution, Tom Paine's book, "Common Sense," the Federalist Papers, and whatever other reading material each individual desired.

They were also told to accept hospitality offered and, upon leaving, ask for only a sandwich (tupperware container provided) and a refill of their water bottle. Like the original disciples, they were sent forth penniless and depending upon the mercy of strangers. In this manner they were much like Buddhist monks. They were also given a pocketknife to whittle designs into their staff when they needed to pass some time in idle pursuits. Both men and women were sent out and the presence of God was so obviously upon them that they were received, welcomed, and joined by all that they encountered.

Those accepting a monastic vow were given a uniform consisting of a white tunic with a red cross from neck to waist, and a long-sleeved grey undershirt that mimicked the chain mail of the Templars. They were also given a sword whose handle was in the shape of a cross. A simple short brown cape reaching to just above the elbows completed the uniform. Granny Muriel presented Kim with the family opal set into a clasp that fastened the collar of her brown cape. Knowing its history, Kim was very grateful to be given such a treasured object.

The flood of converts and recruits gave Kim a good problem and she was soon directing the construction of Citadels and Temple Villages in each state as its membership warranted.

While construction continued apace, the name Kimberly Ryan became familiar to many significant people on both coasts and in the nation's capitol. Her private rail car was not an indulgence but a lure for those who would be allowed the privacy and time to become acquainted, then enamored, of the formidable Miss Ryan as she was informally known. Kim had almost witchy powers of persuasion but these capabilities were similar to those which descended upon the apostles at the first Pentecost. They were more of the Holy Spirit than from witchcraft. Some, however, would be unable to discern the difference.

Miss Ryan's simple message was that America and our good example represents the best that we can do among imperfect humans and institutions but we are in danger of losing it. It follows that many good men and women are needed to protect what must be the shining city upon the hill.

In one Tuesday breakfast talk, Kim said,…

" In the old days, some denominations assumed that if you were wealthy, it was because you were favored by God. It followed that the poor, in some manner, must therefore be sinful. But I say to you, some are born lucky and some are born unlucky. Bad things happen to good people and very nice things happen to some quite awful people. I will have to ask my Father why this is so." (Which Father?)

"It is no sin to be shiftless but it does imply some lack of character. And, character can be learned… if you work at it. As a very young man, George Washington wrote and kept a little journal of traits that he aspired to follow.

In other words, he built his own noble character item by item until he became the paragon that the nation needed at the time that he was needed. As they say, Go thou and do likewise."

This, and many other little talks were what kept the Kim Missions multiplying with good people who did good work wherever they went.

Just as the Shakers were a communal fellowship, so were the Kiministas. Kim did not much like this sobriquet but it was better than "Mission of Shining Knights" as some wished to use to identify Kim's Missions. The Shakers are now known only for their excellent furniture with its uniquely simplistic style. The United Society of Believers in Christ's Second

Appearing, as they were called by their founder, Ann Lee in the 1780's, were a fellowship much like monks and nuns who were celibate but increased their number through an aggressive program of adopting and nurturing orphans. One recent-day Shaker commented that, in the early days, there were many "wintertime Shakers" who joined only for the food and shelter that was available during hard times. These opportunists also added to the Shakers' number as did many women who found equality unlike that of the practices of "outsiders." When the supply of drop-in hobos and needy orphans dried up, the celibate Shakers dwindled down to only three members at Sabbathday Lake, in Maine.

Later that month, in another not-so shining city on a hill, Miss Ryan was prepared to give the keynoter speech at the Republican Governors' conference. Generous political campaign contributions, Kim's well publicized history of good works, her unparalleled powers of persuasion, and the influence of the Lord Almighty conspired to make her laudable reputation come to pass. She began speaking to a skeptical audience with low expectations and concluded with a hall full of enthusiastic and devoted followers. She began...

"....Our Declaration of Independence is as relevant AND

NECESSARY today as it was on July 4, 1776. The entire document is deja vu all over again but I will cite only two brief passages. To wit:

Governments are instituted among Men, deriving their just Powers from the Consent of the Governed, that whenever any Form of Government becomes destructive of these Ends, it is the Right of the People to alter or to abolish it."

and

"But when a long Train on Abuses and Usurpations, pursuing invariably the same Object, evinces a Design to reduce them under absolute Despotism, it is their Right, it is their Duty, to throw off such Government, and to provide new Guards for their future Security."

Kim then said, "Would anyone deny that abuses and usurpations of today's government have become intolerable? Our founders told us that it is our RIGHT and DUTY to change things. What are we waiting for? Do not expect any help from the GOP or DNC. They are the source of the despotism. Term limits are another good place to start. At this point, Kim said, she almost almost quit writing this speech. Mark Levin had just sent her a rough draft of his book to be titled, "THE LIBERTY AMENDMENTS" which had many of the arguments just expressed and also described a methodology for revising the Constitution in spite of the barriers that many will no doubt erect to protect their fiefdoms. Mark's book scared the dickens out of Kim as Mark clearly made the case that we are in even greater danger of losing America than she feared. And, her fears were great.

Kim continued...

"Well, I will soldier on in the war to retake our country. Rome became so debauched that the barbarians were able to take over and we are well on our way to repeating this shameful period of self destruction. I cannot sit idly by even if I know that I can have little influence over the outcome. Still, a pebble can hope that by being thrown into the pond, it might make a ripple. Sadly, too often it will merely sink quietly into the muck. I am that pebble and dare try to make a ripple."

Kim reminded one and all to re-read Matthew 10:34 as they prepared for the end times which were approaching fast. Matthew quotes Jesus as saying, "Do not think that I came to bring peace on earth. I did not come to bring peace but a sword."

Kim continued in a low voice...

"Shakespeare puts words in the mouth of Henry V that may be relevant today even in a highly edited form that I will now quote…"

> *WESTMORELAND states, "O that we now had here*
> *But ten thousand of those men That do no work to-day!"*
>
> *The KING responds, "*
> *If we are mark'd to die, we are enough … and if to live,*
> *the fewer men the greater share of honor.*
>
> *He which hath no stomach to this fight,*
> *Let him depart;*
> *We would not die in that man's company who fears to die with us.*
>
> *This day is call'd the feast of Crispian.*
> *He that outlives this day, and comes safe home,*
> *Will stand a tip-toe when this day is nam'd,*
> *And rouse him at the name of Crispian.*
> ......
> *He that shall see old age,*
> *Will yearly say "To-morrow is Saint Crispian's day."*
> *Then will he strip his sleeve and show his scars,*

And say "These wounds I had on Crispian's
day."
Old men forget;
But he'll remember, What feats he did that
day.

This story shall the good man teach his son;

We few, we happy few, we band of brothers;
For he to-day that sheds his blood with me
Shall be my brother; be he never so vile,
This day shall gentle his condition;
And gentlemen in England now-a-bed
Shall think themselves accursed they were
not here,
And hold their manhoods cheap while any
speaks
That fought with us upon Saint Crispin's
day."

Kimberly spoke to a hushed audience who were moved to the core of their being by a spirit that was more than Kim's words and more than that of this earth.

When Kim concluded, "As Shakespeare suggests, we can but do what we can do, from where we are, with what we have. The Kimberly Mission, in all of its manifestations, may yet be that little band of brothers that makes the difference.

I ask you to support us and to support any and all candidates for office who demonstrate the principles of honesty, decency, and faithfulness."

And, with that, the often all-too dignified delegates burst into cheers more reminiscent of a rock concert than of a political event. The main shout was..."AMEN!"..and, with that, it became apparent that something more spiritual and less political had happened.

A few weeks later, Miss Ryan was invited to an interview of the Fox news show hosted by General Otto Grammler, hero of many battles in the jungles of Viet Nam. Kim agreed with the proviso that her comments would be aired in full and unedited. Grudgingly the network and general agreed.

"Miss Ryan, or would you prefer to be called Kimberly?" asked Otto

"Kim is fine."

"Well, Kim, I notice that your missionaries carry swords and dress like knights of old. What is that all about?"

"We are a secular, nonprofit, charitable, monastic order of brothers and sisters who advocate religious behavior in ourselves and others but, like the Knights Templar, we are ready, willing, and eager to fight evil wherever we encounter it. Like the Guardian Angels who ride subways and confront thugs, we are not afraid to physically confront evildoers."

"Are you not afraid of getting in trouble with the law?"

"That is a problem but many municipalities have deputized us so we have the status of a sheriff or a marshall. We are also in the process of getting Federal legislation to protect not only us but anyone who acts in defense of self or others."

"Kim, how do you justify that?"

"Well, Otto. Our founding fathers had a very tolerant view of justice administered by firearms. Today, we seem content to allow police to find out who killed us rather than to prevent our demise. We need a few gunslingers and the authority to protect the peaceful from the lawless. As for justification, I refer you to the Second amendment and to the first sentence of our Constitution.According to the preamble to the Constitution of the United States, its primary task is to "provide for the common defense."

Kim continued, " Barbary pirates (or Ottoman corsairs) became a nuisance soon after the Muslim conquest of the north Africa in the region of Tunis, Tripoli, etc. Their predation upon the "infidels" reached a peak around 1600 but as soon as Jefferson became President, Congress, in 1801, passed legislation to provide ships to attack the Barbary pirates. The "United States Department of the Navy" had been established in 1789 but they now had the ships they needed. In 1804 William Eaton and U.S. Marine Corps 1st Lieutenant Presly O'Bannon led 8 (!) U.S. Marines and 500 mercenaries to capture Darma, a major city of Tripoli. Hence the first line in the Marine hymn..."From the shores of Tripoli to the halls of Montezuma..."

"The holocaust of 9-11-2001 should be sufficient to convince any reasoning citizen that the Barbary Pirates are again running amok. They have declared jihad so it is reasonable that we need to counter with another Crusade. Our "Shining Knights" do not have the goal of retaking Jerusalem but we accept their motto, "DEUS LO VOLT!.""

"Forgive me, Kim, but I am a simple soldier and my latin is not what it should be."

"The cry of the Crusades, in many languages, was, "God wills it!" We believe that God now wills that we stop enabling evil and the works of Satan and get to work draining the swamp."

"So you believe in a physical Satan?"

"You bet! How can anyone doubt it! His works are manifest and his followers are running rampant throughout the world. It is utter madness that we allow a few ignorant pirates with an outboard motorboat and a handful of AK-47s to hijack a multi-million dollar ship just because corporate lawyers do not allow the crew to arm themselves. To passively allow your employees to be captured to avoid possible litigation is a greater evil than piracy. The desperate pirates at least have skin in the game but the executives and politicians are betting the lives of others."

General Otto might not have been convinced but a large segment of the watching audience were and also began to consider political candidates in a different light. They had been given a new yardstick against which to measure them.

The interview was played and abstracted endlessly and the "talking heads" made Kimberly and her "Shining Knights" a international phenomenon. While unintended, the name "Shining Knights" stuck.

XVII: 2005

Preparing for Battle

~

The 19th-century belief that the United States would eventually encompass all of North America is known as "continentalism." An early proponent of this idea was John Quincy Adams.

In 1811, Adams wrote to his father: "The whole continent of North America appears to be destined by Divine Providence to be peopled by one nation, speaking one language, professing one general system of religious and political principles, and accustomed to one general tenor of social usages and customs."

In the name of "multiculturalism", many today would have us speaking many languages, accepting any sort of religion, from witchcraft to homicidal Islam, or anti-God suppression of the religious beliefs of others, and embracing anarchists and "occupiers."

XVII: 2005

Such "tolerance" is sometimes called moral relativism which is, in general, the belief that everything is as good, noble, desirable, as everything else. The belief that some things are better than or inferior to other things is damned as stereotyping. Kim, and others like her, unapologetically believed that America was destined to lead others and to provide an example of exceptionalism for all nations.

She, and her followers also knew that some things WERE better than others. Just as God is BETTER than Satan. Sadly, some could not comprehend the notion of discriminating good from bad and had even corrupted the use of that word. As well as many other words.

The Kimberly Missions grew so fast that Kim was hard pressed to graduate a "Knight" to preside over each citadel and the village that grew up around it but she found a way. Rather, God found a way, and Kim knew it. Just as the Holy Spirit descended upon the Apostles at Pentecost, so did the spirit descend upon those surrounding Kimberly. She could send them into the world knowing that their message was true and that they would be believed in their call to prepare for a final battle against the forces of evil. Satan had no power against the Kiministas. He had no power over Her and neither could he prevail against her followers

Shadrach, Meshach, and Abednego, devout Jews taken up into the Babylonian captivity, refused to bow down to idols and so were bound and thrown into a fiery furnace. The next day they were seen walking around, unbound in the furnace with a fourth man who was presumed to be an angel protecting them. King Nebuchadnezzar was so impressed by the power of the God of the Israelites that he issued an edict saying that any offense to this God was to be considered to be an act of War. And, Daniel did not do so badly when thrown into the lion's den so Kim's emissaries expected and received the protection that was their due as representatives of the Living God. From time to time, there were a few unfortunate martyrs but they were the rare exception.

Back at the home office, Kim's first act was to establish "Sammy" as the CEO of the whole sheebang, over his objections. In private, he protested, "I am an angel, not a Captain of Industry! You can't make me do this!"

"My friend, you, yourself, anointed me the Child of God. And, you are stuck with it. Besides, who else could I trust? I suspect that you might recruit Michael, and Gabriel, and some of those guys if you really needed a Board of Directors."

"I might just do that." Grumped Samuel. "Don't dare me!"

It was good that Kim had someone with whom she could be herself. They could wonder about how the faithful would deal with the "sign of the Cross" when it became knon that there were, "the Father, the Son... and Daughter...and Holy Spirit" as part of the whole-ness of God. With no one else could Kim even think about such irreverent notions and such was the basis for many comfortable and enjoyable conversations. She with her Diet Coke and he with his holy seegar.

Kim did not fancy herself in need of disciples or apostles but she did need an inner circle of trusted collaborators. She called this the administrative committee and sought out trusted friends from her past. Among these were Sister Baldwin from the convent, Sister Mary Grace from OLPH, Father Lorenzo, her brother, Shawn, Fanny Gorgio, the me-dia vulture, General Otto Grammler, another media hound from the FOX network, Professor Hilbert, from her college days, Sammy, and Michael. These nine trusted associates were, she knew, completely dedicated to The Cause. Knight leaders from vari-ous citadels were brought in as needed to work on local issues but this cadre was sufficient and always nearby when group-think was needed.

Part of the appeal of the Kim Missions was its ecu-menism. Catholics, Baptists, Jews, Hindus, Buddhists, Moslems, or any other faith-based follower was ac-cepted. As long as...they would vow to protect the innocent and to fight evil to the point of physical battle, if necessary. The missions were militant and intended to be triumphant. Part of the vow included an inflexible acceptance of the equality of women (consider who the founder was) and all humankind.

Each Citadel contained a separate chapel for the followers of any faith represented in the local population. Just as Jesus sent his disciples to the Romans, Greeks, Philistines, Irish, and Ethiopians, …and others; so did Kimberly send her representatives to the most far flung reaches of the Earth. In some miraculous way, they were accepted and protected wherever they went. She especially encouraged practicing Jews to join their mission to make the world a better place by actively confronting evil and in protecting the innocent.

From her center in Glenview, Kim sent fourth books, magazines, newsletters, blogs, e-mails and speakers. Everyone knew Kimberly and they loved or hated her, just as they had her brother. The difference was that Jesus was dealing with only about 60,000 square miles (200 x 300, if my arithmetic is correct) while Kimberly had to deal with a world linked by instantaneous communication. Her goal was to have one "citadel" manned by a Knight in each state in the U.S. and one in every country in the world. The power of "The Mission" was so strong and so evident that not even the worst hell-hole of a country could prevail against any Citadel. This fact alone led the Pope to establish a commission to keep watch and report to him, in person, about the activities of Kim, her followers, and the citadels.

Certain Papal Assassins made plans to do away with this source of discontent but they died in such mysterious ways that others with the same views decided that fear was preferable to hostility. Many decided that acceptance and obsequious behavior was called for. Others became converts to the growing cabal advocating sainthood for this remarkable woman.

The Mission Center issued an advisory identifying groups that might wish to consider in coming down on the correct side in the elections of 2008. The Mission had extensive "position papers" covering each of the examples in the following short list and for hundreds of others.

PARTIAL LISTING OF OPPOSING GROUPS

Right-to lifers vs.   Abortionists
Catholic Church vs.   Atheists United
blue collar unions vs. government worker unions
Baptists vs.   ACLU
Evangelicals vs.   occupiers and anarchists
GOP vs.   DNC
responsible blacks vs. Crips and Bloods
Harley Owners Group (HOGS) vs. Hells Angels
conservatives vs.   liberal professors
Nuns vs.   Planned Parenthood

To her private list, she added Ralph vs. Shawn. She was glad to know that Ralph had become a priest but she worried about Shawn who was driven by a consuming need to add to his not-inconsiderable personal wealth. No one could deny that he was a gifted scientist, engineer, and inventor, He was also the darling of and go-to guy for DARPA. (Defense Advanced Research Projects Agency) When they needed a new way to kill something, Shawn was "the man."

There was usually a common breakfast at each Citadel. Via teleconference Kim reminded the Knights of the following:

On Sunday April 24th 1994, Pope John Paul II recommended this prayer be used by all Catholics as a prayer for the Church when he said:

> *"May prayer strengthen us for the spiritual battle we are told about in the Letter to the Ephesians: 'Draw strength from the Lord and from His mighty power' (Ephesians 6:10). The Book of Revelation refers to this same battle, recalling before our eyes the image of St. Michael the Archangel (Revelation 12:7). Pope Leo XIII certainly had a very vivid recollection of this scene when, at the end of the last century, he introduced a special prayer to St. Michael throughout the Church. Although this prayer is no longer recited at the end of Mass, I ask everyone not to forget it and to recite it to obtain help in the battle against forces of darkness and against the spirit of this world."'*

Kim then told her followers that her grandfather and many other fighting men of World War II frequently were given courage by the prayer to St. Michael. She recommended that it be recited at each communal breakfast.

Saint Michael the Archangel,
defend us in battle.
Be our protection against
the wickedness and snares
of the devil.
May God rebuke him, we
humbly pray;
and do Thou, O Prince of the
Heavenly Host –
by the Divine Power of God –
cast into hell, Satan and all the
evil spirits,
who roam throughout the world
seeking the ruin of souls.
Amen.

After pausing to let everyone come back to a business mode, Kim said, that "many of the various martial arts began with monks devising ways to protect themselves on the road." She added, "Remember that I have often referred to Luke but it might be helpful to repeat it as you go into harm's way."

Luke 22:31-32, "And the Lord said, "Simon, Simon! Indeed, Satan has asked for you, that he may sift you as wheat. But I have prayed for you, that your faith shall not fail; and when you have returned to Me, strengthen your brethren."

And again in Luke 22: 36-38, He said to them, "But now, he who has a money bag, let him take it, and likewise, a knapsack; and he who has no sword, let him sell his garment and buy one. For I say to you that this which is written must still be accomplished in Me: 'and he was numbered with the transgressors.' "For the things concerning Me have an end." So they said, "Lord, look here are two swords." And he said to them,"It is enough."

Kim also urged one and all to prepare for the end times which were approaching fast. She suggested that they be careful that Satan did not sift them with his temptations. She also reminded them that Dr. Martin Luther King, Jr. had used a quote from Dane's Inferno that she would use too. "The hottest place in Hell is reserved for those who remain neutral." She added, "Our Mission is to do what we can, with what we have, where we are and keep moving forward until evil is banished and the innocent are protected from whatever is afflicting them."

She then introduced "Sam Angle", the CEO of Mission Enterprises who said that Kim's story of the ancient monks and the quote from Luke reminded him of a humorous story about a small sect of Buddhists who went out into the world carrying nothing but a bowl for donations of food and a tall wooden staff.

When asked if the staff was to assist in walking, the monk said, "No. Is for the bandits."

"How does that help?

"Staff help very much indeed. When bandit approach, we say, "Gro kogmr foo moti reekwtor!"

"Oh! Is that a special prayer?"

"No. Means, stick vigorously applied to nuts is sufficient!"

When the laughing died down, a red-faced Kim dismissed everyone for lunch.

XVIII: 2006

Another Miracle?

~

Kim was on what she called "The Holy Net" linking everyone and anyone who desired to do good works and fight evil. At the time, she was linked to a teenager who had started a very successful movement to gather other youngsters desiring to help their fellow humans. Many, many, others had joined in what was, in effect, a conversation without borders of geography. A bloke from Australia could add ideas that resonated with a nearly naked old man in a mud hut in any jungle in the world.

Granny Muriel visiting and was watching with interest and had just bent over to see the screen a little better when a sniper twitched her finger too soon and hit Muriel instead of Kim. Granny fell as if poleaxed and lay spurting blood from her heart. Kim tried to hold the blood back with her hands but to no avail.

When the paramedics arrived from a nearby firehouse, they just shook their heads and placed the limp lump of Muriel on a stretcher and called, "DOA on scene at 15:35. Transporting to morgue."

"No!" Yelled Kim. "To the nearest hospital!"

"Lady, she is gone. A hospital would be of no use! The morgue it is."

"Listen carefully." Said Kim in her slowest and quietest, voice, "I have an entire law firm on retainer. You DO NOT want to avoid going to the hospital!"

The paramedics had dealt with these types before and knew that they would be fried by their bosses if they ignored a possible lawsuit. So they said, "OK, Miss, do you have any particular hospital in mind? Maybe you know a Doc who specializes in miracles."

"As a matter of fact, I do. Now just get going and I am riding in back with my Granny."

The paramedics winked and smiled at each other. It was no skin off their nose if this crazy broad wanted to take a deader to the emergency room. The OR Docs and nurses could handle her. They dealt with crazies all the time. So, off they went, sirens blaring. Hiram said to his partner, "Hope the sirens satisfies this whacko but don't bother driving fast. We don't need an accident to complicate this mess."

When they arrived at the ambulance entrance, a composed Kim alighted from the ambulance as a gaggle of emergency room personnel pounced upon the stretcher. As they pulled the gurney to the ground and popped down the wheels, Muriel smiled up at the nurses and, with a little groan, said, "Good gracious! That hurts!"

The ER Physician looked at the stunned paramedics and said, "What is with you guys? You called this in as dead and she does not look dead to me!"

The paramedics spent the night writing the reports that they hoped to avoid and provided all sorts of automated records that "proved" that the lady in question was deader than a doornail. The only problem was that "the deceased" was recovering nicely after a bullet was removed from her side, close, but not dangerously so, to her right lung.

The sniper, in the meantime had been handled by Michael, the archangel, who sent her back to the Devil with a note pinned to her coat saying, "Quit it!"

The whole event might have faded away quietly except for the fact that an ambitious reporter and her cameraman had filmed the "death" and what they shrilly called "the resurrection" from beginning to end. They also had two paramedics doing their level best to validate their actions and a group of ER techs with diametrically opposed views about one old lady's health.

Kim's only comment was, "Doctors and nurses do a fine job of dispensing love and doing what they can to heal the hurt. I am grateful for their good work here."

Fanny Gorgio fancied herself to be a crusading journalist famous for discovering the untold story and so she took on Granny's recovery as a special project. Her uncanny luck and perseverance led her to a convent and one Sister Veronica who had been apparently been cured of end-stage cancer by a young novice named Kimberly.

The Kim Missions were already world-famous and now Fanny had the story of the century! "Young Missionary Raises The Dead!" screamed the largest possible type ABOVE THE FOLD! The vultures pounced and the hounds bayed and Kim had to go into hiding. And where better to hide than deepest Africa.

The hopeless and helpless inhabitants of one of the worst refugee camps in central Africa looked up one fine afternoon to see 20 white cargo helicopters with red crosses on their noses approach. They were not invited and they did not ask. The Kiministas just came. Upon landing, they got busy setting up a field kitchen with long tables. Running out parallel rope-lines, it soon became apparent that the people were to line up for...something.

The helicopters were Boeing CH-47 Chinooks, called "the Jolly Green Giant" by troops in 'Nam. They were bought on the surplus market from the Air Force "boneyard" and were saved from the wrecking ball for a modest investment. The greens were 51 feet long and their rear loading ramp made them ideal for the type of humanitarian efforts that the Kiministas carried out anywhere and everywhere. They had several fleets of them as well as a Gulfstream 550 with a range of 6,750 miles. It carried 14-19 passengers and required two pilots. At a price of 53 million, it was a bargain because it allowed Kim and her staff to show up almost anywhere, anytime.

Abu-al-Bobo would not stand for these infidel interlopers entering the territory he controlled by faith and fear. He quickly called for Muu-al-Mooki to take them out with an RPG. Unfortunately, the rocket launcher exploded when the trigger was pulled taking off al-Mooki's head and shredding several encouraging onlookers.

The Kiministas looked up briefly but went quietly about preparing a stew of Kansas City beef, Oregon potatoes, (spelled as Dan Quayle would) and California carrots and onions. Experience had taught them to have no fear as they went about their business of doing good works.

Abu-al-Bobo then sent a 5-man squad to flank the interlopers. When nothing happened after an hour, al-Bobo sent a scout to hurry them up. The scout came upon a squad of skinless bones whitening in the sun. The scout recognized the clothes and weapons of his friends but the skeletal remains scared the Hell out of him. (literally) al-Bobo refused to believe the trembling and babbling report and gathered a 20-man detachment, armed to the teeth, that he, himself, would lead. After a 21-man pile of bleached bones was later inspected, there were no more oppositions to mealtime.

The camp was so large that five serving lines were set up and a Knight, in full ceremonial dress, stood at the head of each handing out an aluminum bowl and large spoon to each person. He, or she, said, "You must say, Thank you America, to have your bowl filled."

The creative pronunciation of this simple sentence brought smiles to the servers but hungry people learn quickly. As expected, one iconoclast took it upon himself to say, "DEF TO AMERIKEE!!" Without a pause, the server looked questioningly at the next child in line who quickly said, "Tank-koo Amireeka!" He got his stew while the holdout only got the satisfaction of stomping on his bowl and stalking away.

The next day, the holdout watched as the first set of helicopters flew away just as an equal number emblazoned with the familiar red cross but also the initials "KFC" landed to take their place. It was the first time that many of the campers had eaten fried chicken with mashed potatoes and gravy with an ear of corn, but they liked it!

The second set of helicopters also brought a large flock of Templar doves which were set free and seemed happy with their new home. The doves also brought comfort to the very incognito Kimberly as she dished out the chow along with everyone else who had been instructed not to recognize her.

The familiar rotation of helicopters followed day after day. By this time, the worldwide media had arrived and, never missing an opportunity for product placement, so did corporate sponsors. KFC was followed by Taco Bell, and the refugees soon learned the delights of a foot-long Subway sandwich, a Full-Moon bar-b-que, and on and on. The holdout finally gave in when a fleet of helicopters emblazoned with the words "Happy Meals" arrived. He did so much want to be happy that he has able to cheerfully say "Thamkee Amerekee." He loved the quarter-pounder and fries but did not quite know what to make of the Disney characters that were included. He did, however decide that they were pretty interesting.

Soft drinks were provided at the end of the line and Pepsi soon demanded equal space with Coca Cola, who got there first. Kool-aid had been there from the start but soon Yoo-Hoo chocolate drink and Mountain Valley spring water from Hot Springs, Arkansas, and a veritable cornucopia of drinks was winging its way to this remote outpost in Africa.

The ever vigilant newshawk, (or, might we say newsvulture?) picked up the spoor of the Mission feeding activities and, following the flight plans, arrived unnoticed with the third set of meals on wings. Gossip and chatter soon led Fanny and her cameraman to the bones of the aborted assassination attempts which were duly filmed, exaggerated, and shouted to the world.

"Good Grief!" Was Kim's response, "Will that meddlesome woman ever stop stalking me and mine? Probably not. Sammy, what do you say about giving her a interview so she can get the facts and philosophy right?"

Among many other things, Kim told Fanny that an important function of the missions was to love and comfort the hopeless just as they were doing in this remote corner of the world. She alluded to several similar efforts in process but firmly told Fanny that these locations would not be revealed because publicity would be contrary to the reason for doing these things. She and Sam attempted to give Fanny's scattergun approach some direction and they offered to tell her about their philosophy.

And so they did. It helped some but hyperbole was in Fanny's DNA so the next round of sensational pronouncements had only some elements of truth. That was about all that Kim expected so she got back to her main interests which were doing good where it was needed.

Other food service establishments, some out of goodness and some out of marketing passion, followed this model and soon refugee hell-holes all over the world were being succored. In their tent after a hard day's work Kim commented to Sammy, "Not a bad 30th birthday present to me."

"Way to go girl! What is next?"

"This is almost trivial in the overall scheme of things but our logo is all over the place and often looks too much like the emblem of the disaster relief 'Red Cross.' Let's have a designer standardize it so that it consists of four equal arms with a short bar at the end of each. Sort of like four T's."

"O.K., What else is next?"

What next was being decided in the Vatican. Pope Jonathan III turned from the TV to his ever-present priest and said, "I must see this remarkable woman. Send a cable asking her to visit me. Wait! Would I ask Jesus to be at my beck and call? I am almost convinced that she is, indeed, His Sister. All the reports, and there are many, suggest that she is more than just....what? I don't know! Tell Her that I will come visit her. No, just ask her very politely if we can meet."

XIX: 2008

The Elections

The Democrat nomination process ended up with a popular African-American Senator, recently a community organizer, who told a questioner on a "rope line" that he intended to "Spread the wealth around." The GOP selected Major General Lukas ("Hopalong") Cassity to run against him. "Hoppy" got his nickname from jumping out of one too many airplanes into the thick of combat. He, too, was African-American but he was as ebony as his opponent was tan. A roaring capitalist, he opposed his opponent's ideas about creating paradise for the poor by sending the people's money to Washington to then be doled out to those that the bureaucrats deemed in need. Cassity was only a reserve general and his "real job" was building large wheeled machines to move earth around or do other useful work. Such men make good Presidents.

After retiring from the Army and before becoming a "Captain of Industry", "Hoppy" served
a brief stint as a classroom teacher and then as a
civil servant and soon came to realize the essential
difference between tax-funded organizations and
for-profit enterprises. To take a simple example; if
you wanted a pencil in a government job, you must
convince someone that you would use it to do good
things, meet mission goals, or please someone. In a
for-profit job, all you need to do is show them you
will use the pencil to make a buck.

Cassity frequently quoted Margaret Thatcher,
the Prime Minister of England from 1979 to 1990, as
saying,"The problem with socialism is you soon run
out of other peoples' money." He was ably assisted in
his campaign by the Amazon Governor of Ohio who
had squeaked into office and then balanced the state
budget while reducing taxes. The widespread happi-
ness in Ohio was only marred by the weeping and
whining of union bosses and teevee watchers who
rose from their couches only to walk to the mailbox
for a welfare check. Governor Maria Soliz-Santiago,
one-time lettuce picker turned worker's activist,
knew poverty and she knew the value of hard work
to restore ones' sense of self-worth. In an unheard
of and outrageous move, she managed to pass laws
that, in effect, gave each person's welfare check to
an employer who would give the person on the dole
a job. Businesses got free labor and the poor who

needed a job got one. She also opened "commissary stores" with wholesome but basic products that could be redeemed with "food stamps" that were good nowhere else. These stores sold plain clothing, generic food products, and everything that a Wal*Mart might have but only one or two of each type. No alcohol, tobacco, or other luxuries were available but one could buy beer. Non-alcoholic beer!

Delinquent children in Ohio were quickly removed from the influence of unfit parents and moved into Stepford-type villages where crime was nonexistent and life was as close to 1950's suburbia as contracted Disney imagineers could make it. Use drugs in Ohio and...POOF!...your children were sent to a happy place.

The screaming liberals of Ohio were shouted down and often physically assaulted by those who saw hell-holes become pretty nice places. A clever law made it lawful to assault obnoxious people or bullies. Just as the duels of old made for civil behavior, so did the "no fault" assault laws teach spoiled and aggressively offensive people that there might be consequences to their behavior.

With such a running mate, how could Cassity lose? They were bright, innovative, conservative, Black, Hispanic, female, and just plain nice folks. Of course, old Lucifer was hard at work and turned out his usual minions by the millions. But Cassity had Kimberly and Her minions also working just as hard to keep her beloved nation from heading down the wrong track.

After being sworn in, Cassity went to work with a vengeance. He did his level best to undo the "nanny state" that led bureaucrats to believe that they had a right to tell everyone else how to live their lives.

In his first press conference, President Cassity said, "Our Constitution says, among other things, that it was established to "secure the blessings of liberty to ourselves and our posterity." We have gone a long way down the road to DENY liberty to our citizens and this stops today! Under my watch the EPA will not declare a puddle in someone's backyard to be a "wetland" that they control. Citizens will have the liberty to use their own property as they wish! And, this goes for every other agency that usurps property rights. Coal miners and mine owners will have the liberty to mine and sell their coal without government interference. Fishermen can fish and little girls can sell Kool-aid in their front yards without having to beg some functionary for a permit to open or run their business."

"There will be a Cabinet-level Department of Regulatory Management that will work tirelessly to ensure that any regulation proposed or in place will function to benefit citizens and the nation. Any crackpot who tries to force his or her ideas upon everyone else will be quickly join the ranks of the unemployed. This department will be staffed with ordinary citizens having no connection to Government. These part-time, and well-paid, consultants will use the common sense that is the main characteristic of the American people to do that which bureaucrats seem incapable of doing. They will review all regulations and bring, to the attention of auditors or legal experts, those that appear inappropriate or just plain wrong."

"All office-holders will be asked take an oath attesting to their understanding that they are Civil SERVANTS whose purpose is to assist citizens and serve the interests of the nation as a whole. To this end, I will ask Congress to pass a law ending the practice that a government job is an entitlement to be held without regard to competence or performance so that the buffoons, scoundrels, and money wasters can be routed out and sent packing."

"I will also ask that the exchange of favors or money for favorable legislation be made a Federal crime and that lobbyists be allowed to provide guidance and advice but nothing else. I will propose that all conversations between legislators and lobbyists or campaign contributors be recorded and made public on the internet."

"Finally, I will do anything and everything that I can to stop wasting taxpayer's money! Spending millions on "research" to prove or disprove what should be obvious to anyone of sound mind will end today…if…Congress will give me and every legislator the right to question and delete any line item that is not of obvious benefit to the nation or its citizens."

And with that, the howling mob was off and running. Everyone wanted, as the old "China Hands" used to say, "to protect their own rice bowl." Hoppy and Maria looked forward to having a gay old time rooting out special interests and substituting worthwhile endeavors for the madness that had become standard practice. Maria said, "Let's see if we can get rid of the lunatics that are running the asylum."

Hoppy nodded and said, "They ain't seen nothing yet. Round two will be coming up soon. By the way, we need to take time to thank Miss Ryan and her mission folk for their help in getting out the vote. The GOP finally got smart and made the election about our values and not arcane theories about capitalism that no one understands or much cares about. Let's give people jobs instead of yammering about how they must appreciate the theory that helping millionaires will cause the rich to want to create jobs. This might be true in some way, but there is no way to skin that cat that the kitty will enjoy."

Later that month, President Cassity met with the Speaker of the House, Sally Fassor, and said,"Sal, we need to steal a base from the opposition who are always sniveling about the minimum wage. They only do it to get the votes of the supposed vastly underpaid. Who are the most underpaid workers in the U.S.? Soldiers! That's who! They want to raise the pay of burger flippers but no one has any interest in our warriors. Why don't you get your gang together and whip up a law to raise the pay of any member of the armed services to a minimum of $10.50 per hour? And raise the pay of all enlisted personnel by a corresponding amount from where they are now."

"Lucas, that is a wonderful idea! When we spring it on the opposition, they would not dare vote against it! We will just have to be careful that they do not get wind of this and claim that it was their idea."

"Good deal, Sal. Now I need to toddle off to the Pentagon. I am going to get the Joint Chiefs to help me work on the wording to amend the rules of engagement for our warfighters. The battle-field etiquette that has evolved makes out troops sitting ducks. The can't shoot unless shot at first.

They can't shoot if some quote...innocent party... unquote is in the neighborhood. And, they are hauled into court and tried for murder if something goes wrong. After I work it out with The Chiefs, I will be back to get Congress to make it law."

Cassity continued, "First, I want our soldiers to consider themselves to be conquers from the moment they cross the borders of anyone designated as the enemy. And, by the way, I expect Congress to identify "the enemy" whether groups or nations. That is your job."

"If they are there to conquer, they must be ready to shoot to kill. It must be a requirement that they will disarm or destroy anyone not designated as friendly. The rule is simple, do no harm to friends; do all harm to enemies."

"If we give them a weapon, we can not, must not, pass judgement on how the weapon is used. Troops must be indemnified against any judgment or punishment regarding how it is used. We can no longer send them in harms way and then try to second-guess how they carried out the mission. The rear echelon mothers ("REMs") have been second-guessing front-line troops for far too long."

"I propose that the only crimes for which soldiers may be tried are rape and theft for personal gain. To my way of thinking, "midnight requisitions" of stuff needed to accomplish the mission should be within the bounds of creative initiative."

Sal grinned from eat-to-ear and said,"Lucas, you get the Chiefs to write it up and bring this to me and I will see that it gets through. It is good to have both Houses of Congress firmly in our camp so we can do things without the usual backstabbing and political sabotage."

XX: 2009

Armageddon : A Holy (?) War

~

President Cassity invited Kimberly to the White House for an extended visit in order to get to know this remarkable young woman with the huge following. After all, she had helped him to get elected.

At age 32, Kim might no longer be called a "young woman" but she was still a handsome, even beautiful, person who had a beatific presence that brought calm and serenity to any group, from two to two hundred. Her distinctive habit of tunic with the red cross was worn without affectation and so it seemed suitable for any occasion and even just right for her. Her wide smile, dusting of freckles and the few strands of grey in her bangs, made her instantly likable even before she began to speak.

"Mr. President, I would like to introduce my special friend, Sammy Angle. I hope that you do not mind that I took it upon myself to invite him to share your gracious hospitality but I need him and I think that you will be glad that you met him."

"Glad to have him join us. As I mentioned, this is not a formal visit or even an official event. It is all quite off the books and this is not easy to arrange. Like everyone else in the known world, I have heard quite a lot about you and your mission. I believe that your followers are called Kiministas?"

"Well, yes. We had to call our little band of do-gooders something and Templars was already taken."

"Hardly a little group, would you not admit?"

"Well, we HAVE grown, by the grace of God, and with luck and pluck.

However, it distresses me that, after a certain point, the dragon seems to want to run away with the rider. But then, Mr. President, you must be all too aware of this problem."

"Yep. My minions often seem to want to use my name to achieve their hearts desire. The only solution is to get good people, give them clear guidelines for what is needed to be done, and let them run with it. Like you say, sometimes the dragon runs away with the plan and crashes the crockery like a bull in a china shop."

"This is why I have Sammy. He can juggle all the balls and, while keeping them in the air, knows which ones are made of glass and which ones are made of rubber."

Sammy grunted and said. "More like juggling a batch of chain saws along with a litter of kittens!"

"Very good, Sam!" Said the POTUS. "Can I use that one? It seems quite apt."

And so the three of them spent a quiet afternoon talking of this and that, of ships and sails, and sealing wax, and cabbages and kings. But no one offered to take little oysters for a walk along the seashore.

They met Maria Soliz-Santiago and Kim and Sammy liked her immediately. The POTUS later said that they should not even consider "dressing for dinner" because they were to eat in his private quarters. This did not matter because, while they had several changes of clothing, what they wore was exactly like what they could change into. Well, not quite.

XX: 2009

Among the recruits to the Kiministas was one Eve Saint Sansinne, the famous stylist. She insisted that a little variety in the white tunics would be welcomed by the women in the group. Men did not care what they put on, the simpler the better. In any event, Evie soon wore Kim down and a light pink tunic with a scarlet satin cross became an acceptable alternative. Worn with red rough buckskin boots (engineer-type or cowboy), the outfit was still recognizable but, at the same time, quite stunning.

The President was very impressed with the new style and Kim reminded herself to pass on his reaction to Eve. Evie might be a knight but she still was a professional in her trade and would be tickled pink to hear that her suggestion had found favor in The White House!

President Cassity said that he was aware of the excellent work that Shawn Ryan, while only 28, was doing for DARPA (Defense Advanced Research Projects Agency). Shawn had more gadgets in operation than even Lockheed's famous "Skunk Works." The POTUS, perhaps showing off a little, even mentioned that he was aware that Father Ralph Ryan was now the assistant pastor at OLPH.

Kim had to admit to herself that she was so busy ministering to the world that she probably neglected the relatives who she loved very much. She vowed to spend more time with them.

Kim decided that the POTUS did not seem to have any ulterior motives for inviting them to visit and she believed that, like Billy Graham, she could be a spiritual sounding board to a President. She also felt, with her special empathy, that Lucas Cassity needed a friend that he could talk to in confidence and with honesty. Well, she could do that.

And so, their visit became the first of many and soon Kim and Sammy were dropping in to visit every few months. Recently, their conversations turned more and more to the unrest in the Middle East and the calls for Jihad from many sources. Kimberly took these apocalyptic threats more seriously than the POTUS because she had friends in High Places (higher even than the White House) and knew what was coming. So, it came to pass that Kim, Sammy, and the POTUS were enjoying a nice summer evening on the Truman Balcony overlooking the south lawn when they spotted four tiny dots of a HALO (high altitude, low opening) parachute team streaking downward and popping their chutes just over the Washington Monument. With great skill they took turns steering their chutes so that each was speared on the pointed peak of the monument. One by one, they slammed into the side and spread out so there was one on each side of the obelisk before simultaneously detonating the explosives they wore on their chests.

"My God!" cried Cassity, "They blew the whole top off that thing!"

Before anyone could even think of moving, an RPG streaked into the East Wing and blew a hole wide enough to drive a tank through. That may have been the intention because the next event was a torrential storm of light tanks parachuting down onto the South Lawn. Only then could the Air Defense Command perceive an armada of advanced stealth cargo planes blanketing the sky from horizon to horizon dropping tanks and wave after wave of paratroopers onto the mall from the Lincoln Memorial to the World War Two Park.

As Cassity was hustled into the White House and down into the secure basement war room, Kim and Sammy were momentarily left to fend for themselves. She felt, rather than saw, a battery of six "Quad-Four" guns pop up on the roof and start throwing shells downrange into the massed tanks and troops sorting themselves out. For the uninitiated, a quad-four is a set of four 50-caliber aircraft machine guns linked together to swivel to and fro and up and down as aimed by a gunner sitting in a bucket seat between the guns. The gunner needed a padded helmet to avoid deafness and a radar-operated gunsight made the whole assembly very destructive of men or equipment.

The rain of hell from the "Q-4's" was awesome to behold and Kimberly stood transfixed as the Secret Service belatedly grabbed her and Sammy and trundled them down into the shelter. Not the President's place that was in full war operation, but a bunker secure-enough for civilians.

"Are we the only ones being hit?" Asked Cassity.

"Nope. They are attacking Dallas, Denver, Detroit, and Disneyland in Anaheim." said General Hickenlooper, the Army Chief of Staff.

"What's with all the D's?" muttered Cassity. Neither then nor later did anyone have an answer to that question.

"You will be happy to know that they are also attacking New Orleans! No "D" there!" Said a Master Sergeant assigned to the CIA who had seen it all. "Sir, We got ourselves a real shit-storm here and no advanced warning at all!"

As the enemy tanks rolled down Constitution avenue, a flock, a very large flock, of drone Zeppelins swarmed toward them from Andrews Air Force Base. The D-Zips, as their inventor Shawn Ryan called them, resembled a fire plug in shape and size with four delta wings, two vertical and two horizontal. These lighter-than-air machines fired two kinds of weapons. For tanks and such, they fired a "sticky ball" about the size of a golf ball that pasted itself to its target and then flowed out to form a circle about the size of a manhole cover which then ignited to burn like a thermite grenade or magnesium flare through the shell and into the interior causing the vehicle's own munitions to detonate in a spectacular manner.

The second weapon was a "man net" which was used against personnel from a couple of fighters up to a platoon. When fired, it unfurled to form something resembling a circular fishing net about 50-feet in diameter. The strings of the net functioned like primer-cord in that they were a very powerful explosive that, when detonated, reduced whatever was in the net to very tiny particles.

These "Black Hole" weapons were stored in vast numbers throughout the United States and only the President and DARPA knew of their existence. General Hickenlooper's only comment was, "What the hell is that? Where did we get those? Do we have a lot of them? Enough for Dallas, Denver, and wherever?"

"Yep." said the Sergeant from the CIA who was a man of few words as benefitted his profession.

"Now watch this!" said the President with pride and glee. He pointed to the closed-circuit screen that showed the entire ground armada burning merrily away while horrified soldiers cowered as explosive nets continued to rain down and make mincemeat of their comrades. The few surviving enemy fighters were puzzled to see things that looked like shop-vacs on treads roll up and command them, in their language, to "Strip! Now! From helmet to shoes! You have thirty seconds!"

When the first soldier hesitated, his chest blew open from an explosive bullet, as did the second, and the third. There was no fourth. Uniforms flew and boots were tossed and soon an army of nudists were all that remained of the invasion force. The "Fido-Robots" as Shawn called them, marched them away over the hill and they were seen no more.

Months later, many Mideast nations were visited by Boeing C-17 Globemaster III cargo planes whose clamshell rear doors opened to return their citizens, thoroughly debriefed, but without briefs, by way of parachutes. Nearly all of these naked skydivers had only once before used a parachute and were being given on-the-job training as they were shoveled out of the planes that flew off over the horizon without a backward glance. The G-III had plenty of counter-measures and self-defense systems so no one foolish enough to interfere.

By the way, a new invention allowed the return-
ees to be put to sleep and permanently dyed light
green before they were sent home so attempts by
them to enter certain countries was not a likely opportunity in their future. A similar procedure, but
blue in color, would eventually be applied to incor-
rigible American gang members and career criminals. This threat alone was sufficient to prevent
second offenses in all but the most hard-headed of
criminals and wannabe felons.

XXI: 2009

A Visit to the Vatican

~

Kim's brother made a surprise visit to her headquarters. He had never been there and was astounded by what his big sister had done with her investment from the lottery. He had seen photos of her fleets of nurturing helicopters and her private train car and her private jet but he had no idea that she was so very wealthy.

"Hi, Sis. It looks like you are a big-time tele-evangelist now. And, by the way, I like your outfit."

"Did you come here to mock me, little brother? Or, should I call you Father?"

"How did you get so rich? A multimillion dollar lottery only goes so far. I am not complaining, mind you but just curious."

"I took a vow of celibacy, not poverty, Padre brother. You would not believe the business empire that backs up this whole enterprise. We live communally and monastically but are very active in the real world, preferring to be out passing out blankets to those living under bridges than chanting hymns of praise. We are also very involved in politics believing, as we do, that certain individuals could never have managed to get elected without help from certain dark forces working behind the scenes. How, for example, could a serial adulterer go from infamy to honors just by applying the simple tactic of stalling and lying until he arranged to have himself protected by the self interests of his political allies? At least some of these allies must have been influenced by the Devil himself."

"They say that Satan can present a beautiful countenance and can offer many blandishments to tempt the weak. One of The Mission's incidental jobs is to put some backbone in some of the weaklings in Congress. This is why we are so active in politics and why I make time to visit President Cassity, who I am proud to call a personal friend. Not for a quid-pro-quo on either side but just for companionship and to discuss mutual interests. We both feel that our country needs a lot of saving after the last half-century of governmental self-interest has changed what our honored founders tried to do."

Ralph said, "I am impressed by what you have done and what you hope to accomplish and so is someone else. To my surprise, I was visited, in extreme secret, by Bishop Malrooney last night. He wanted me to carry a message to you in a most surreptitious manner inviting you to visit Pope Jonathan III without ceremony and world-wide hoopla."

"Gee, brother. I don't know if I would fit that into my schedule…"

Watching Ralph's stunned and horrified expression put Kimmie back into a state of girlish glee as she remembered how she had so often used her innocent little brother as the victim of her most fiendish trickery. Oh, but she did love him so much so she did not let him suffer long.

"I love the expression on your face, Ralphie! Of course, I would be most honored to meet the Il Papa, as the Italians call him. He is head of my faith. I am, after all, a Catholic even if my mission is ecumenical and made up of members of all faiths. The "All Religion Alliance" is a serious subtitle of the Kimberly Missions and we are gathered together to form a united force against the forces of evil and their handmaidens, the unbelievers. I am in no position to set conditions but please ask that my friend Sammy accompany me and that meetings will be between only the three of us with no advisors or sycophants present."

Father Ralph, picked up his cell phone and, in a minute, it was done. Kim said, "Ralphie, you and I and the Pope all have the same calling. We must love, guide, and protect our flock."

Since Kim had her own jet and the Vatican had its own air terminal in Rome, A secret trip was no problem and Kim and Sammy were soon whisked through the bronze doors of Pope Benedict's private auto entrance off the main street into the Vatican. After a courteous interval to "wash up" and sleep off jet lag, Kim and Sammy were shown to the Pope's private quarters where a light lunch was waiting for them.

Pope Jonathan III was a big, not fat, man whose six-foot frame more closely resembled that of a fullback than the monk that he had been. With a big smile, he grabbed Kim's hand and shook it before she could courtesy or kiss his ring, as tradition demanded. "My dear Kim," he said, "This is a private meeting between us servants of God. Nothing that the nuns taught you applies here. And, this must be Sam, your right-hand man."

Sammy accepted his hand for a hearty grip. He knew God so a mere Pope did not impress him but he liked this fellow, nevertheless. "Please call me Sammy, Papa."

They dined upon a nice shrimp cocktail, a perfectly baked potato and a thin slice of nicely seasoned lamb. After strawberry ice cream, which the Pope said was his special "temptation," Jonathan mentioned Father Ralph's good works as an Assistant Pastor and spoke of the good reputation of Kim's parents in the OLPH Parish and then said,"And, as far as your Grandmother Muriel is concerned, I really enjoyed reading her Dachau Devotionals. I have recommended this book to all the nuns in the Vatican. Sister Maggie, as your Grandmother called her, is a good example of what the religious life requires from time-to-time.

Il Papa quietly enumerated what he considered to be miracles attributed to Kim. The miraculous cure of cancer in Sister Veronica, the resurrection ("Please do not deny it. The evidence is there.") of Grandma Muriel, the saving of the souls of Sister Fortuna, now Sister Mary Madeline and Gloria Costello, and the miraculous appearance of the "Templar Doves" at the time of her birth, and thereafter. "So, you see, Kim, I have quite enough to have you beatified right now. How would you feel about being called The Blessed Kimberly? If you remember your catechism, this is the third of four steps toward canonization. "

He continued, "As Pope, I can officially recognize that you should be canonized because you have practiced Christian virtues in a heroic manner and, as Pope, I am protected, by the Holy Spirit from error in this opinion. You may then be called the "Blessed Kimberly" or the "Venerable Kimberly." Unfortunately, I cannot call you "Saint Kimberly" until you have been dead for five years. I will assert publicly, in the next Papal Audience, that I have sufficient proof that this will happen in the course of time."

"By the way, not even your mother could deny telling the Pope the conditions of your birth and the part that your friend Samuel had in it."

Sammy sat upright in his seat as if someone has lit a firecracker under him. "Kimmie, Should we give him the full show?" Sammy asked with a mischievous grin.

Kim replied, "As Pope, I supposed that he is entitled."

Jonathan III was seldom mystified by things religious in nature but he could not see where this was going and said so. "I have gone way beyond the bounds of tradition here and you two are talking it as if I am discussing some minor deal here." J the III was beginning to feel grumpy.

Had he mistrusted these ingrates? Were they the charlatans that all his advisors had warned him about?

"Sir," Kim said soothingly, "We need to know about your health. Are you strong enough to stand a shock or might you have a heart attack if subjected to something really extraordinary?"

"Why! Are you going to set off a bomb or something? Are you a secret Muslim terrorist with an explosive vest?"

Kim said soothingly, "Have no fear, Jonathan, you are going to see something no man has ever seen and something that only a Pope should see. Sammy! It is showtime!"

With a soundless explosion of radiance, Sammy became Samuel the Archangel.

The Pope, stunned as he was, heard a pounding on the door of his chamber and a shouted, "Sir! Sir! Is everything all right in there? We see an intense light from your windows and coming under the door. Should we come in ?"

Recovering quickly, as Popes learn to do, Jonathan said in a voice loud enough to be heard over the knocking, "Everything is fine. The lamp that my guests brought as a gift is pretty bright. Don't worry. We will be a while yet."

The Swiss Guards had seen no gifts carried in nor would they see a lamp later but their job was not to question the whys and wherefores of the leader of the Catholic Church.

"I gather that you must be the Angel Samuel that appeared to the Virgin Kate? I must admit that you look rather like I suspect angels should look but I suppose that is because you get to choose to appear as we expect?"

"Yes sir. That's about it."

"Well then, that seals the deal. I WILL announce the canonization and reveal the evidence that we have collected. I will even suggest that you be called "The Venerable Kimberly" or, "The Blessed Kimberly" on formal occasions. By the way, what are those two doves doing on the balcony?"

Taking a few steps, and looking more closely, Jonathan III said, "They seem to have a cross on their breasts. Are these the Templar Doves I have heard so much about? How did they get here all the way from America?"

"I don't know, sir." Said Kim, "They even showed up while we were feeding refugees in Africa. They are not everywhere but they do show up in the darndest places at the strangest times."

"Hm, like the dove that showed up when Jesus was baptized by John?"

"Don't know, Sir. They never say anything, just coo."

Samuel interrupted, "If you don't mind, I would like to slip into something more comfortable. But, before I do, I would like to give our friend Jonathan a little souvenir of our evening."

With that, he pulled a flaming sword from its scabbard and lay it on the marble floor, carefully away from the carpet. "That should cool down in a few minutes." And, when it did, he placed it across Jonathan's lap saying, "See that little nick on the edge? I got that when I broke Lucifer's sword before God locked him up. But now, he is threatening to break out again. This is why Kim is here. You would be wise to listen to her suggestions."

"By the way," Sammy continued in his ordinary aspect and puffing on his "holy smoke." "You might refer to the sword as a relic that was found in your archives. The truth might get you impeached or whatever it is they do to Looney-Tunes Popes. If you ever get around to building a church named St. Kimberly and Samuel the Archangel (and you will) you can hang it over the altar without provenance."

By this time, everyone was tired and they departed to their own apartments after agreeing to meet the next day to tour the Vatican museum after breakfast. Jonathan said, "We will close it to the public and spend all day with a knowledgable guide. The Sistine Chapel alone is worth seeing but half of everything that Michelangelo did is around here somewhere. That and every other renaissance artist and those that came before and after.

And so they spent several days in companionship. At dinner on the last day, Samuel, or Sammy, instigated a serious discussion.

"Well, that was the best meal I have had yet but, before we part, we need to think about a few things. First, we are an angel, a Pope, and…arguably…a saint. So, we should be on a first name basis. Jonathan, who was the first Pope?

"Peter"

"And, who appointed him?"

"Jesus."

"So you are the inheritor of the business Jesus started? Right?

"You could put it that way."

"And, who...or what?..Is Kimberly"

"I really don't know.!

"Well," said Sammy, "I announced to the Virgin Kate that Kim would be born, without sin. And, her father was?... Prompted Sammy.

"God?" answered Jonathan, beginning to feel very uneasy about where this was headed.

"Indeed!" said Sammy. "Now we get to the crux of the matter. The Church is the work of Jesus. Right? And God was his father... and I think we can agree that God was Kimmy's father."

"Now hold on, just a dadgummed minute!" said Pope Jonathan III.

"So," continued Sammy, "That makes Kim, Jesus' half-sister. Different mothers, same Dad! Ipso-facto, abracabradabra! So, technically, the Pope works for her."

"Hold on there!" Shouted Kim and Jonathan simultaneously.

Kim said, "I will go first! Jonathan, I do not want your job, which you do very well. I want to be your friend, not your boss. I may be Jesus' sister but I am your daughter. And, like all daughters, I will speak my mind from time to time but, for now, we better forget all about the Saint Kimberly business. Let's just go with Sister Kim of the Kiminista Missions for now. If you want to refer to me as the "Blessed Kim" from time to time as you recognize our good work, that would be fine with me."

And so, the Papal audience for the public that week was very complementary toward Miss Ryan and the good work being done by the Kiministas and their Mission but the notion of sainthood was shelved, for now.

XXII: 2012

A Landslide Election

~

The newly reconfigured Republican party, supported by the Fellowship of All Benign Religions (FABR) spearheaded by the Kim Missions, won in a landslide. The issue was clear: believers against unbelievers and worshipers against those who celebrate secular emptiness. And, lovers of God vs. haters of outsiders.

The new President, actually Lucas Cassity starting his second term, made a point in his inaugural address to demand that Congress formally declare war against "Fundamentalist Muslims who fail to deny that they are at war with America." He said that Congress must first admit the problem and then take action.

He accused Congress of cowardice by expecting the President to take full responsibility and demanded that they admit that "a state of war exists."

He also suggested that mobs celebrating bombings in America and Israel be targeted by ICBMs without warheads but with sufficient clout to leave a vast hole where the joyful crowd had shouted their approval of the murder of innocents. The merrymaking following the collapse of the World Trade Centers would never again be allowed. He also suggested that "collateral damage" was acceptable when the damage was to those who choose to associate themselves with killers and tyrants. His "scorched earth" policy caused the liberals and other America-haters to fall down frothing at the mouth but the nation in general, and the vast majority who elected the President, were tired of begging those who hate us to love us.

He also requested a formal ban on the practice of "Sharia Law" in the United States. And insisted that Congress immediately end all foreign aid or payments to nations that allowed Christians to be attacked and their churches to be bombed. Similarly, those who exploited women, gays, or other minorities (especially Jews) would receive no funds whatsoever from this nation.

Although it took several months for these ideas to percolate through layers of officialdom, the final, and briefly stated, result was that homicidal dogmas and all of their consequences were outlawed.

He continued, "On the local front, the children and spouses of all police officers, firefighters, and other "first responders" killed in the line of duty should be guaranteed that the paycheck of the man or woman who supported them would be continued, without diminution and without taxation, as long as the children were under the age of 21. If there were no children, then for as long as the spouse remained unmarried. They should also receive free medical coverage."

He added, "These provisions should also apply to the families of soldiers killed in action or in training and military members wounded in action to the extent that they are unemployable in the profession that they left behind."

Members of Congress and other "leaders" who objected were told that, unless they could prove that the Government never wasted a cent on less worthy causes, they should just shut up and pay up. Many voters believed that such craven officeholders were unworthy of their position and most were never reelected.

Kim and Sammy were back at "The House," as they called it, several months after the POTUS had

issued his challenges to Congress and were again
enjoying the view from the Truman Balcony.

"You are off the a great start, Mr President. There
is nothing like having both Houses of Congress in
your party to get things done." Said Kim

"Yep. Your brother, Shawn, deserves a lot of credit
too. There is nothing like winning a war to get the
citizens on your side. Seeing tanks rolling down
Constitution Avenue was a mighty clear wake-up call."

Cassity then said, "Now we need to bring harmo-
ny to the warring factions within our own borders.
If you read the Federalist Papers, you can clearly
see that the greatest fear of our founding fathers
was that a democracy could be torn apart by what
they called "Factions." We call them "special interest groups" but the idea is the same. A group becomes unalterably convinced that their notions are
the only right, just, correct, or sane positions and
that anyone thinking otherwise is deluded or evil."

"Months ago, you put out a pamphlet discussing,
in detail, the issues that fascinate some of these ac-
tivists. I tore out the table of contents and saved it.
Want to talk about these issues again?"

"Sure." Said Kim, "Hand it over to refresh my
memory."

Right-to lifers vs.	Abortionists
Catholic Church vs.	Atheists United
blue collar unions vs.	government worker unions
The Institute for Justice vs.	ACLU
Evangelicals vs.	occupiers and anarchists
GOP vs.	DNC
responsible blacks vs.	Crips and Bloods
Harley Owners Group (HOGS) vs.	Hells Angels
conservatives vs.	liberal professors
Nuns vs.	Planned Parenthood

"Well," said Kim, "The membership of our missions just about cover the left-hand column. The 49-51% nation got a seismic jolt from the invasion but, like 9-11, it probably will not last. Our side is now about 60-30 with 10% who don't care. The problem is that we have too many people who unconsciously believe that the sun rises and sets only to keep them in day and night. The Missions are doing everything that we can to convince people that there is a "Higher Power" than themselves."

Cassity said, "When jihadists killed about 3,000 innocents in the Trade Towers and the Pentagon, America was briefly united and treated Iraq to a taste of the "shock and awe" that we can bring to those who attack us. Unfortunately, craven politicians and progressives and lefty "journalists" immediately set out to undermine President George Bush for political reasons and sometimes just for the hell of it."

Kimberly quietly said, "From my perspective, I see the hand of Lucifer in some of this. They do not have to believe in Satan for him to use them as tools to achieve his ends. Not all fools and mischief-makers are slaves to The Devil, but no one should believe that none of them are."

"Some believe that puny humans are important enough to change the temperature of the Earth. Others, often the same ones, believe that everyone else must say and do what they consider appropriate. For example, do they not see that it is insane to think that anyone has a right to tell everyone else what size soft drink they should purchase? In California, Oregon, and similarly progressive places, people assume a "right" to tell everyone else whether, and how, they can mow the lawn, or use their fireplace, or what they can do on their own property."

"Lists of the notions of self-identified do-gooders that result in oppressive regulations and laws would fill many encyclopedias. If they still made encyclopedias. Can you believe that California is enduring a self-imposed drought and going without water to drink, bathe, or grow crops just because a bunch of loud fanatics want to keep some minnow happy and fruitful? How can one fight such brain-damaged philosophers? It is like the "whack a mole" game! Just as soon as you whack one, another pops up. Or, often the same whacko pops up with a new and different nutty demand."

"Kimberly, some of us must be grownups and decide. The "moral relativism" that assumes that everything is just as good as everything else is bunk! Some things are better than others and some people are better, smarter, and more worthy of imitation than others."

"And some religions are superior too!" Kim said. "At least, as practiced, if practiced properly. And, this is a huge "if." No one will deny that the Inquisition was a very bad thing but the Catholic church soon abandoned this practice. Too late for my role models, the Knights Templar, and Joan of Arc, but the Church meant well, in a medieval and backward sort of way. Hopefully, Islam will one day abandon its ignorant, backward, and deluded practitioners and become the religion that it could be."

"But, I digress." Kim said. "At this point in time, Christianity is far superior to Islam, at least as it is being practiced by the jihadists and those too cowardly to speak out against their fellow Muslims."

"The original Crusades were called for by those who believed that the "infidels" were persecuting Christians in the "Holy Land" and Jerusalem. Today, we do not need to rely on rumors as they did in those days. We can see the Christian churches being attacked and burned to the ground on the six o'clock news!"

"Well Kim, I can promise you that no foreign aid will be sent to nations who allow such outrages. Congress did pass the formal Declaration of War I asked for. It applies to nations, groups, and individuals who not only overtly participate in attacks on the U.S. and its citizens, wherever that may be, but on THOSE WHO ENCOURAGE, INCITE, OR RECOMMEND acts of terror or murder, kidnapping and other felonious acts. I must inform Congress and obtain their consent before physically landing troops in foreign lands but I am given blanket permission to overfly and launch attacks from the above.

"This means drones, bombers, stealth critters of all kinds and…ICBMs.

The Air Force can also use the Lockheed AC 130H ("Spectre") gunship which is based on the big ole Hercules. It has four gunners firing side-mounted cannons with 40mm, 105mm, and 25 mm rounds. In brief, it can circle a target for hours and shred anything up to the size of a small city."

"So," concluded the POTUS, "I have the authority and the equipment to take care of business overseas. More importantly, I have the will to utterly destroy those who would destroy us. During the cold war, General Curtiss LeMay headed the Strategic Air Command whose motto was "Peace is our Profession" and, thanks to his B-52s, The U.S.S.R. was afraid to start "the big war." LeMay was fond of saying, we can reduce their cities to rubble and then make the rubble bounce."

"Kim, I need your help in another war. I know that you have your hands full with your various and sundry relief missions and your responsibilities as shepherd of your flock but perhaps you can suggest someone who can help me to deal with criminality? Something has to be done about gangs, drug dealers, slavers, and all of those unsavory creatures that infest the underworld. And, I am not going to neglect the white collar criminals who inhabit the executive suites of skyscrapers."

"As a matter of fact, I can suggest someone."

Sammy, who could almost read her mind, shook his head and said, "Kim…Kimmie!, don't even think about going there!"

"Mr President, my friend Michael is very interested in fighting evildoers and is a sworn champion of goodness and justice. He has been retired for some time and out of the country for a while."

"Far, far, away." muttered Sammy. "In outer space, you might say."

"Please ignore Sam, Mr. President. Michael has sort of been in the Army, actually something like the CIA, so don't expect him to provide too much in the way of identification papers and a resume. All of his paperwork burned up while he was off fighting a bunch of rebels."

"Then it is settled Kim. Your recommendation is good enough for me and I can have my staff whip up all sorts of identification papers for him. I will also give him a little card that says that whatever he needs is approved in advance by me. This sort of thing can really cut the red tape and mow down interfering bureaucrats."

Sammy seldom joined in the conversations but as they were leaving, he said, "Speaking of fighting crime. Remember the way you dyed the invaders light green before returning them to their countries? This might work with hard-core repeat offenders. Let them know that, after the second serious offense, they will be dyed light blue so that people will know to keep a wary eye on them." With a shrug, he added. "Just a thought Mr. President."

"And a very good one, indeed! We will have to think about how it might be implemented."

Eventually, the POTUS and Congress put the "Racketeering Influenced Corrupt Organizations" (RICO) Act to good use. Congress formally designated all illegal drug importers and major distributers to be part of a worldwide RICO. Gangbangers were also deemed to be a RICO and sent to GITMO Dos, high in the Andes. Young gang wannabes were summarily shipped off to escape-proof villages for "Honorable Citizen Training."

RICO was also applied to hackers, identity thieves, and other technological criminals. Prison sentences were mandatory and the practice of hiring these gifted troublemakers as "security consultants" was put to an end.

XXIII: 2017

The K-Missions Industries

~

A 500 million dollar jackpot gave the K-Missions a good start but a fleet of relief helicopters, a Gulfstream Jet, private rail car, citadels and associated villages in each state, etc., etc. do not come cheap. So, how did she do it all?

By 2017, Kim was 41 and her enterprise had adopted, and abandoned, several names and trademarks to finally settle on K-Missions Enterprises (KME) and K-Missions Industries (kMi). The latter was the cash cow that kept the former running. In addition, about half a dozen billionaires and a few sponsors who were mere millionaires wanted to share in the good works. Kim insisted that they could contribute to their heart's content and suggest as they will but they had no control and had to sign formidable legal papers to that end.

From selling a few templar doves to the complex conglomerate that it had become, kMi concentrated on things that could be manufactured. Such as the "Templar Runabout" which was a sports car quite frankly and unashamedly modeled after the 1950's MG TF. Upgraded, of course, to include a self-stowing hardtop, modern electronics and convenience and safety features that were expected as the norm. It came with one of three types of engine: all-electric, gasoline, or natural gas.

This led to the requirement for service stations to fuel these critters and the "service" was back in the stations to 1950's standards. It took a heap of string-pulling in Congress to relax and revise regulations but kMi Energy Stations once again became an entry-level job for the nation's teenagers. This, of course, led to the need for drilling for, refining of, and transporting petroleum and natural gas. Then coal was added and, after more Federal arm twisting, the coal industry was restored after being nearly destroyed for no good reason other than to placate envirolunatics.

The "Holy Net" that replaced tracts and pamphlets and books led to the development and manufacturing of laptops and desktop computers created by the geniuses of all varieties that wanted to be associated with the K-Missions.

The Missions began as a quasi-monastic order but they, too, evolved. Everyone associated with KME and kMi was required to join the order and take an oath "To serve God by serving humanity and fighting evil in all of its manifestations." They also took vows of poverty, community, and service.

A member of the K-Mission could serve as a Knight, wearing the distinctive habit (white tunic with red cross, and long-sleeve silver undershirt), or as a priest (Catholic, progressive, Buddhist, or whatever), or Monk or Sister of the Mission. The last two were cloistered and stayed around a specific citadel and surrounding village to serve and support them while the two former groups were very much out and about in the world.

Among the services provided by each citadel was a "Prenatal Center" that provided the pregnant with an alternative to abortion. Their motto was, "give a little time to save a life." Women could stay (or, if need be, "hide out") until an inconvenient child was born and then raise it or offer it for adoption. Nearby was what was once called "an orphanage" but was, in fact a home for the recently born or those snatched (the Knights were militant, remember?) from the misery of unfit parents.

A minor source of funding was the "Un-Tattoo Parlors" at each citadel that used a patented methodology to remove the evidence of drunken or ill-advised youthful marking that was later a source of regret or undesired distinction. This methodology was offered, free of charge, to penal institutions who wished to forcibly remove "gangsta" markings and had passed laws allowing them to do so.

Obviously, membership boomed and confidence in kMi products swelled after the Pope let the cat out of the bag, so to speak, but most members of the missions had already decided, by observing her works, that Kimberly was a saint.

XXIV: 2017

The Pope Explodes a Bombshell

~

Kim was in her office quietly noodling about what to do next when Sammy burst through the door. "Quick! Turn on the TV! Now he has gone and done it!"

When she saw who was speaking, she said, "Sammy, what is Jonathan saying?"

"Never mind! Back it up to the beginning. Here, let me do it!"

Samuel grabbed the control; and zipped back to the opening as Pope Jonathan III began,

"Several years ago, I met a remarkable young woman. Her name is Kimberly Ryan. We spent three days together in informal companionship, visiting the museum, and talking about this and that. We decided to keep secret the nature of our interactions but recent evidence has changed my mind. I have spent a week in prayer and contemplation and have finally concluded that, as leader of the Church, I must speak out."

"What I have to tell you will cause the earth to wobble on its foundations and will cause an international uproar. However, I have concluded that I was given the job I now have to bring this message to you and so I must do it. Here, and now."

"My priests have helped me document all of the steps necessary to present the evidence that will be available in printed form, and in several languages, later today at each Catholic church in Rome. Such widespread distribution is necessary because the demand for "THE EVIDENCE" will be great. But I will summarize here and now."

"Earlier this week, I just happened to meet a priest who gave me information that made all the difference. Father Lorenzo was the young Kimberly's Priest at the time of her First Communion and Confirmation. As most of you know, the latter is the time when young Catholics complete their former baptism and "are sealed with the gift of the Holy Spirit."

"Father Lorenzo informed me that young Kimberly was marked by stigmata at the time of Confirmation.

The blood marks or scars of Christ on the hands, feet, and side are imitative of the crucifixion and the first recorded stigmata were exhibited by Saint Francis of Assisi but over 300 recorded instances have occurred since. Most importantly, almost all have been associated with sainthood or the designation of Blessed."

"In addition to the evidence I have documented, there were things about the meeting between Kim, me, and her associate that must remain under the seal of faith. But I will tell you that, as Vicar of God's Church, what will be forever unsaid convinced me that this young woman is not only Blessed but is most assuredly a living Saint. Tradition requires that a person be dead for five years before sainthood is bestowed upon them but this is merely a formality that is sort of the book of etiquette for this kind of thing. So it can be set aside and I do so here and now. For reasons that will be presented in written form later today, I declare Miss Kimberly Ryan, to be Saint Kimberly."

"Good Day, and God Bless you."

When the image of Jonathan III was turned off, the entire world went nuts! Sammy turned to Kimberly and said, "Boy, Oh boy. Now it begins

What also began then was the writing of the "Epistle of Saint Kimberly" which continued until after the "Great War" of 2020.

XXV: 2018

The Apocalypse

~

Lucifer also knew immediately of the Pope's pronouncement. We will not specify whether he uses cable, dish, or something far, far different. In any event, he cried out, "To Arms! Let all hell break loose!"

And, it did.

In Washington state, the ecofreaks came out in droves to protest logging.

On Wall Street, the occupiers swarmed the area again.

In California, a strong earthquake tore the Pebble Beach golf course asunder and created widespread disaster in that region.

In Washington, D.C., the Amalgamated Union of Federal Workers walked off the job demanding a 25% raise. The wheels of Government ground to a halt and most citizens and their property were temporarily safe from regulators.

In Oregon, The CHILDREN OF TERRA marched with their placards:

THERE IS NO GOD IN THE SKY
ONLY THE CHILDREN OF TERRA

and

THERE IS NO DEVIL UNDER GROUND
ONLY CHILDREN OF TERRA ABOVE

and

EACH INDIVIDUAL IS THE
BEGINNING AND END OF IT ALL

That such nihilism was insane was lost on the enthusiastic mob that talked only to each other and kept their thoughts circling around the same old drain until their world view became the only one that they accepted as reasonable, even profound. They might be coo-coo but they could cause much commotion and damage.

In Iran, Mahmoud Ahmadinejad shouted from the rooftops that he had a nuclear bomb mated to a long-range missile and Israel would soon be no more. In Israel, the jet engines started turning over. Soon Tehran was no more.

Along the Mexican border, narco-gangs poured across, overwhelming an outnumbered and out-gunned U.S. Border Patrol that had been emasculated by politicians seeking Latino and liberal votes.

The Taliban began to stockpile explosive vests from sea to shining sea and brainwashed U.S. citizens were raring to blow themselves up.

The Satanists turned out in droves carrying a black flag with a golden goat's skull rampant. Kim had seen such an emblem on Gloria's thigh many years ago. It had brought her back to reality just in the nick of time. Why they selected Austin, TX is not known but there was a large and active coven already in place at the U of Texas so, why not?

The long-extinct Yellowstone caldera began to simmer and worried the Devil out of vulcanologists who knew that this area was, long, long, ago the site of the largest volcanic explosion in Earth's history.

The Reverend Jeeter Jackson, joined, for some mad reason, by the Klu Klux Klan, began attacking the Kiminista Mission and its citadels verbally at first and then, increasingly, physically based upon some cockamamy theory of heresy that was not coherent enough to try to refute. The Knights made short work of them.

In the new President's war room, she watched each event pop up on the threat map and wondered why she had agreed to follow Lucas' suggestion that his Vice-President run on the platform of carrying on the good things that he had started. She picked up the direct line and shouted! "Hoppy, get your ass over here and help. I have a whack-a-mole situation happening and I need help!"

"Now, Maria," Lucas said, "the Soliz-Santiago clan would expect you to take charge. After all, The President, has all of the resources in the world…"

"Be quiet, Hoppy, Just get over here! And, ask your witch buddy to come along too."

Lucas Cassity was not too happy to hear his friend Kim called a witch but Maria was under a lot of strain and this was not a battle that was worth squabbling over. So, he and Kim were soon on their way to the White House.

Kim took time to inform all citadels and their leaders to prepare for the worst and asked each draft a one-page plan to combat the threat nearest their center. She specifically suggested that the California citadel use the big KM Chinook helicopters to start ferrying large water bladders from the streams of the Sierras to the Monterey Bay area.

When they gathered in front to the situation map (shown below), they saw that it was indeed a whack-a-mole situation. They had natural disasters, looney-tunes protests, anarchists, and terrorists popping out all over like smallpox on an unvaccinated victim. And, speaking of terrorists, another red circle bloomed in the middle of Iowa as they were watching.

figure 3:
Map of "Hot Spots"

"What was that?" yelled Maria. the POTUS.

"The University of Iowa was just leveled by ten or more jihadists with explosive vests." Said Captain York, "Why Iowa, I don't know. Why the University, I don't know either but I have a team taking off from Chicago as we speak. They might know something in a couple of hours."

"Speaking of Jihadists," the POTUS said, "What is happening in Iran?"

"The Iranian SAMS are in the air but the Israeli Air Force is more stealthy than we knew and should reach the Cruise missile release point any minute now."

"Well, we can clean up that mess later. Or, ignore it. But, it looks like the Caliphate will be put on hold for a while."

Kim said, "Some members of my mission there report that the Iranian students and democrats are out in the streets protesting the theocratic regime. I have given the K-Missionaries permission to join the antigovernment protestors with drawn swords. More knights are being flown in later today. Most governments won't let citizens have guns but swords have been overlooked everywhere. Too Eleventh Century, I suppose."

"I am afraid that I can't give you permission to involve your people Miss Ryan." Said Maria in full POTUS posture.

"Well, Mrs. President. I am afraid that you have no authority over the religious mission that I head. The old freedom of religion thing, you know, and the First Amendment. Remember...Congress (and you) shall make no law prohibiting the free expression of religion. The Kiministas are expressing our beliefs in Iran right now and those who are trying to overthrow the religious fanatics are very appreciative of the help. We are doing what we can here and abroad. The Satanists in Austin are certainly our business and that little brush fire is just about snuffed out. One of our associates, Michael, showed them the error of their ways and dispersed them... widely"

"One perspon, Kim?" Said Maria.

"Yes, Ma'am. Remember the Texas Ranger rule? One riot, one Ranger."

"Miss Ryan!" said the POTUS, "You certainly are a take-charge kind of person. Yet, I suppose any help would be appreciated. Was the Pope right? Are you the Child of God? The half-sister of Jesus?"

"Like that cartoon character Popeye used to say, I am what I am." Said Kim. "That is about all that I am willing to say on my own."

Maria Soliz-Santiago glanced over toward the window and said in a wondering voice, "Isn't that curious? There is a funny little pair of doves with red breasts sitting on the window sill."

Kim said nothing and Lucas, with more information, was speechless.

XXVI: 2018

Natural Disasters

~

The new areas of smoking sinkholes at Yellowstone were a natural disaster waiting to happen but the earth-shattering eruption had happened millions of years ago and, hopefully, it would be millions of years in the future when the inevitable massive eruption happened again. It was in God's hands and Kim was happy to leave it there. The current uproar was, she suspected, the work of other, perhaps Satanic, hands but she was sure that those hands had been slapped and the mischief stopped.

The Pebble Beach earthquake, on the other hand, was just part of the Earth's business and little quakes were so familiar to the people of the Monterey Peninsula that they seldom stopped stirring the scrambled eggs when a tremor hit. This time however, it was a rip-roarer and water, gas, and electricity were out of service and few roads were left passible.

The golf course at Pebble Beach always was interesting. One hole even required that the golfer tee off on one side of a cliff and sail across the ocean to land on the green on the lip of another cliff. Well, now engineers estimated that seven bridges would have to be added to cross the fissure that split one side of the course from the other. When the Country Club recovered, golfers would love the added challenge.

In the meantime, the Kiministas were hard at work helping first responders and utility fixeruppers to get things back to normal. Watering stations had been set up at Carmel Mission, Fort Ord, the Presidio, and the airport. The KM Chinook helicopters were kept busy ferrying water in from the streams of the Sierras to the KM water purification plants that the Kim Missions frequently used for refugee camps all over the world.

The Customs House Plaza, older than the United States, was littered with sail boats of all sizes that were thrown up from the marina by a minor tsunami. Most would never again flit about in Monterey Bay but Honey Bear number 4 would be resurrected to the beauty that she was in the 1930's. Some of her sisters were reduced to kindling. Boaters 1, golfers 0.

The familiar white tunics of Kim's followers were now mixed with the new pink habits that had been created by a fashion maven turned monk. As an aside, among the Kiministas, girl-monks were also called monks.

As Monterey was getting back to normal, Kim gathered up Sister Baldwin, Fanny Gorgio, and Professor Hillbert and set off with several helicopters full of Kiministas and needed supplies and equipment to Iowa City to see how they might help the collegians still digging out from the rubble. Kim's old mentor, Professor Hillbert, was expected to be helpful in talking to the egg-headed academicians that they expected to encounter at the University. As it turned out, the Iowa professors were the most down-to-earth folk that one would hope to encounter. Except, of course, if one strayed into the topic of Hawk-eye sports. On this topic, everyone, scholar or lummox, was a worshiper of all sports and their divine players.

The Kiministas' tunics, pink or white, were soon seen everywhere pulling or pushing or cajoling or encouraging as the need required. Especially hard hit was the Lindquist Center because they built it with a huge elevator that was needed to lift the computers back when these things were big. Five suicide bombers rode the elevator halfway up before detonating. This once-proud measurement research center was blown to smithereens and the rubble then pounded into pebbles. The campus gay, lesbian, and transgender center was unscathed. An oversight that the homophobic Muslims would not have appreciated. If any were left.

With several of the the residence halls wrecked, many students were relocated to a swine farm on the outskirts of Iowa City. The accommodations were not all that much inferior to the rooms that some students abandoned but had the advantage of a decrease in the noise level generated by modern electronic musical systems.Thus, studying increased because of the peace and quiet and the fact that there was little else to do.

XXVII: 2018

Bi-Costal Protesters

～

In Kirkland, Washington the local chapter of "Trees First" gathered together the items that they would need to wreak havoc upon the loggers that they detested. They intended to drive spikes into trees so that the high-speed chainsaws of the loggers would rip apart, flinging shrapnel everywhere and, if the tree-huggers were lucky, back into the face of the operator of the saw.

They also had flares to use to start forest fires that would deprive the lumber yards of the product that they needed. That providing boards for homes was a more desirable goal than destroying the very trees that they intended to save was a detail that these geniuses were not capable of factoring into the twisted logic of their philosophy. Their placards with artsy slogans and no-talent art were not very useful as weapons when the Homeland Defense Force arrived en-masse and rounded up the lot of them to be tried as terrorists. The "Children of Terra" in Portland fared no better when the swat teams swarmed their riot and arrested them as vandals and hooligans. Fortunately, recently passed laws made violent protests very much illegal.

That left the occupiers and their tent city on Wall Street that had made a garbage dump of this center of capitalism. They were doused with a nontoxic but permanent pink dye and left to explain their color to parents, employers, and welfare offices with instructions to issue no checks to pink people. Shawn Ryan was pretty proud of this nonlethal solution to crowd control and even more amused by the fact that this "permanent" stain could be removed if the "pinko" showed sufficient remorse and made proper restitution by "sweat equity."

XXVIII: 2018

Lucifer's Lunatics

~

The nationwide gathering of Satanic followers included valid citizens of Hell, punk kids looking to "get lucky", and everyone in between who did not mind being associated with the father of all evil. They flowed into Austin from the four points of the compass and proceeded to engage in an orgy of uncontrolled insanity. No perversion was overlooked and no crime was unexplored as they overwhelmed the police with sheer numbers. Anyone capable of reason and still functioning within the bounds of sanity simply gave up and fled the county. This included the police and the entire state government.

The entire University of Texas was abandoned after the month-long orgy of Satanism so it was easy enough for the entire congregation of evil to gather for one final rite at the Texas Longhorn football stadium. It was not quite filled to the brim as for the usual game but it was packed enough so that the roar of the crowd shook the skies as the Mistress of Ceremonies dragged a nude coed onto the fifty-yard line where an alter was set up. It was already dripping with the blood of sheep, chickens, and various creatures but they had finally found a virgin to sacrifice as the ultimate tribute to the closing ceremonies. God only knew where they would disperse to when they departed. Well, in fact, He did.

As the struggling maiden was tossed unto the altar, the entire sky above the stadium exploded with a brilliant light that was the Archangel Michael, the warrior angel who is the greatest of the first among beings.

He spoke in a voice more mighty that any stadium speaker saying, "I am Michael the Archangel who defeated Lucifer, who you worship. Observe this struggling creature in the sack I am holding. It is your master!"

Michael was so large that his wings stretched from goal-line to goal-line and the sack was like something that might hold a tiny rat. Which it did.

Reaching in, he withdrew a squirming snakelike beast with horns and hoofs in man-shape. "Behold! Once again, I have defeated him and will return him to Hell along with those he brought with him from that pit of nothingness."

With that, he stuffed Lucifer back into the sack, tied a cord around it, and threw it down onto the bloody alter from which the quick-thinking virgin had long since fled. The altar exploded into incandescent fire as did each and every citizen from Hell sitting, standing, or fornicating in the stands.

The wannabees leapt away from the smoldering and charred remains scattered here and there in the bleachers and stadium seats. To say they had the Hell scared out of them and the fear of God put into them would be an understatement. There, floating above them like a balloon from Macy's Thanksgiving parade was an angel looking, in every way, just an an angry Angel should look. The audience was stunned and rendered incapable of movement. They were waiting for the next shoe to drop. So, Michael lowered the hammer.

Michael then said,"Today and, by your recent actions, all of you have earned a place in Gehenna. For the less literate of you, that is Hell. You have also been blessed to have seen the power of The Almighty demonstrated to you so it is not possible for you to doubt that there is Ultimate Good and Ultimate Evil. You have chosen the latter but, if you turn away from evil and, most importantly, make restitution, you have a chance to avoid eternal damnation. Don't even bother to ask how you might earn salvation. That is for each of you to discern and you are a long way from where you need to be so get started by leaving this place…NOW!"

And so, that little problem was solved as the stadium was emptied faster than if those who were fleeing the scene had their hair on fire. Which, was, in some metaphysical sense, true. Many also were in desperate need of a change of underwear.

An unintended consequence to ridding the creatures from Hell in the Longhorn Stadium should have anticipated. Thousands of cell phones recorded snippets of Saint Michael's actions so that the whole event was broadcast to friends of attendees and to friends of friends and to the media with the result that the whole world had definitive proof of the existence of Angels, the reality of Hell, and the possibility that they might be in dire need of salvation. Millions of souls were "born again" that day/evening or at least had the fear of God put into them.

The out-of-control Federal Workers' Unions were handily handled by President Maria who said that the jobs of strikers would be offered to qualified workers on a lowest bid basis at the beginning of the following week. Anyone not at his or her workplace by Monday morning would have been assumed to have resigned and the job would be placed in the "help wanted" section of the local paper. Those holdouts who later changed their minds learned that actions have consequences and that a bell cannot be un-rung.

XXIX: 2019

Drugs: Users and Providers

~

The wealth, power, and influence of so-called drug lords and the gangs associated with them were the result of the demand by the addicted. Whether the users were "sick", evil, or weak-willed is immaterial. The fact is that they wanted/needed addictive substances and were willing to pay any price for them created wealth and a strong motivation among "the underclass" to sell drugs. For those with no hope of a job or even a future, the prospect of becoming filthy rich was irresistible

Those who call drug use a "victimless crime" have never had a young daughter sell her body for dope or a son swept up in a drug bust and forced by the police to choose between jail and the role of an informer with a high probability of being killed as a "snitch." Families and the addicted have been financially and emotionally destroyed while drugs are blatantly sold, without fear, on street corners and in nooks and crannies throughout the nation. The deck is stacked against the police by ineffectual laws that make the huge rewards of dealing punishable by negligible consequences.

In Spanish, the expression, "galena o plata" means "lead or silver." That is, take a bribe (silver) or a bullet (lead). The Latin gangs are so powerful that the threat replaced law and order with police either on the take or looking the other way. In the United States, the excuses were many and the results insignificant.

With lawlessness rampant on the Mexican border and the U.S. Federal Government more interested in Hispanic votes than in protecting the borders, it was only a matter of time until the drug gangs on both sides of the borders combined to create a "no-man's-land" of lawlessness that stretched from Brownsville, Texas to Tijuana across from San Diego, California. What quickly followed was an army of narco-gangs that vowed to regain the lands stolen from their "rightful owners" by the Gringos. They intended to accomplish this by attacking towns on both sides of the border.

Did we mention that narco-gangs were ruthless and fiendishly dangerous and unafraid of any attempt to control them? Those who fear nothing, care for nothing (even their own life), and will do anything, are very difficult to control. They just don't give a damn. Like a snake, they are soulless and deadly and all you can do to stop them is to kill them. But, we have been unwilling to do that so we could not win.

President Maria Soliz-Santiago took the bit in her teeth and rammed a law through Congress that declared certain classes of individuals as "soulless criminals" and that, if without souls, they were not part of the human species. It followed that the taking of their life was not a crime or even much of a sin. With her background, she could not be deemed racist or anti-Hispanic so that usual argument was spiked. She then got Congress to declare an act of war upon "terrorists who invaded our borders." Later, there would be useful "unintended consequences" regarding Muslim infiltrators but, for now, it was sufficient to call out the National Guard in Texas, New Mexico, Arizona, and California with retired President Lucas Cassity heading up the effort.

Kim and her Missions attacked the problem from the other end by setting up addict rescue centers in each citadel and providing love, hope, and therapy. Especially love. Most users were trying to fill some emptiness in their soul and the

Kiministas offered "agape," that is, unconditional love prompted by a connection to the love that flows from God. Many new "guests" were quickly disabused of the notion that all love was linked to eros, that is sexual love. Many soon came to realize that a pal offered more comfort than a bed partner. Did we mention that the Knights of the Kiministas were militant? That would explain why many in therapy were snatched off the streets and out of the gutters, literally and figuratively to enjoy the love and hospitality of the K-Missions. The cure-rate was "miraculous." What else would you expect when Kimberly was involved?

Meanwhile back at the front, General Cassity organized the formidable and underutilized might of the fighting forces of the U.S. of A. We had the goods, but often not the will to do what was needed. In this case, a sweep ten miles wide on both sides of the border began in Brownsville and swept north like a column of army ants on the march. Anyone with a weapon or drugs was shot on the spot. Not since judge Roy Bean and his "Law West of the Pecos" was justice as sure and swift as that administered by General Cassity. As soon as they passed on, the government was returned to the locals with a reminder that corruption had been declared a capital crime and that the armed forces were able to return as quickly as they came.

POTUS Maria Soliz-Santiago saw that Congress followed up on the military action with fences and other deterrents erected by the U.S. Army Engineers. Foolproof photo ID cards with biometric verification (fingerprint or retinal scan) were required of everyone crossing any border and applying for any job. The location of legal immigrants and visitors was verified weekly. Vigorous followup was applied to any discrepancy with the result that transnational terrorists were blocked completely.

The motto of "peace through surrender" was replaced by "peace through vigilance." The corollary, "With quick action when necessary" was assumed. The military budget was rooted in the preamble to the Constitution which states:

We the people of the United States, in order to form a more perfect union establish Justice, insure domestic tranquillity, **provide for the common defense**, promote the general Welfare, and secure the Blessings of Liberty to ourselves and our Posterity, do ordain and establish this Constitution for the United States of America.

Maria had her work cut out for her in untangling the loss of liberty that had resulted from the actions of regulators and bureaucrats who tried, with too much enthusiasm, to implement the laws that resulted from legislators attempting to buy favors, votes, and cash in envelopes which were dropped off in the dark of night.

The first goal of the President was clear and documented in the Preamble. So, before her first term was up, she set in motion everything that would make America the greatest military power on earth. With no fear from external forces, she directed her second term toward protecting the innocent from those already within our borders. The events of the last few years, both military and supernatural, had gone a long way toward convincing those who exhibited bad behavior of the more violent kind, that they would end up in the graveyard or in Hell, or both unless they changed their ways. It helped that about 15 sitting Senators and 143 Representatives had become little piles of ash by "mysterious forces." Their replacements had a heathy fear of avenging angels of the type made famous by the Texas Stadium videos.

Kimberly was a frequent and most welcome visitor to the White House and she told Maria that it was about time for the final act in the war against evil.

XXX: 2020

Armageddon

~

And so it came to pass that Kim, Maria, and Sammy were once again enjoying the Truman Balcony that, by now, was surrounded by 5-inch ballistic glass that could stop anything up to and including an RPG. Kim pointed out what appeared to be a tornado approaching from the East and a bank of luminous fog from the West. That they were on a collision course was obvious.

Kim said in her usual calming voice, "This is the final battle. The Armageddon. Lucifer knows that it is hopeless but it is the final chapter and his fate. He has gathered all the dark angels in Hell and is facing the Heavenly Host. Tell your Secret Service that you do not need to be dragged off again. You are perfectly safe with me. and this is something that you need to see. I even flew in a special guest, in absolute secrecy on my jet and invited him to join us."

Kim stepped to the door and returned with the most recognizable man in the world. "Madame President, I would like you to meet my special friend, Pope Jonathan the third."

"Your Holiness" said the Methodist Maria, "I hope you will excuse my lack of familiarity with proper protocol but welcome to the White house."

"Thank you. Kim is not much on protocol either. She refuses to let me call her the Blessed Kimberly or even Saint Kimberly which I ordained her to be."

"My, Oh My" Said the POTUS, "Kim, You naughty girl. You never told me about all of this."

"Well," said Kim with her usual modesty, "I have brothers who prevent me from being too high and mighty.

"But", protested Jonathan, "You are indeed high and mighty and to deny it is false modesty. A venial sin to be sure, but unworthy of one who has accomplished so much."

Armageddon

At this point, Sammy, sitting quietly in the corner in his bowler hat and brown suit, said "If you folks will excuse me, I need to go help my companions."

And, with that, he stepped off the balcony, popped his golden wings, acquired his angelic aspect and, waving a flaming sword, flew into the approaching white cloud just as it merged with the tornado. Day turned to night and the stars came out as the the forces merged with the sound of a million chain saws meeting a million buzz saws. The din was horrific and lightning flashed from cloud to cloud, white to dark and swirling vortex against all-enveloping light.

Kim, Maria, and Jonathan watched, transfixed as the white cloud flashed internal streaks of lightning and the grey tornado threw off flames then they swirled together and the grey faded to nothingness. The fog dissipated, leaving a beautiful twilight sunset. Samuel returned and handed the Pope and POTUS each a foot-long perfect white feather. Samuel the Archangel said, "These broke off in the battle. You can keep then as a souvenir of the final battle between good and evil. Satan and his minions will no longer be able to interfere or influence events. Bad people will have to be bad on their own."

XXXI: 2020

Peace on Earth

~

From the First K-Mission Citadel, Saint Kimberly sent a joint message from her, Pope Jonathan III, and President Soliz-Santiago that the world was currently at peace and they expected all nations to cooperate to keep it that way. America's might, the Holy Mother Church, and the will of God would help to maintain the peace of the world.

And, by the way, Kimberly announced, Jesus was returning next Wednesday to celebrate Passover in Jerusalem. The world was finally fit for him to visit and he would drop in on the Pope, the POTUS, and finally, his sister Kimberly.

Following this announcement, whole nations were converted. Those with Christian leaders went first followed by some few of other sects but everyone who had seen the Texas video, and few had not seen it, were ready to sign up to the proven religion. Parliamentary governments fell and changed leaders and many others scheduled immediate elections to elect believers of their God as the chief executive.

Saint Kimberly had informed one and all that the one true God would share dominion with other divinities. Not all were, however, acceptable. Those with homicidal leaders and followers would not be allowed access. Their followers were urged to convert.

The "Evidence" distributed by Jonathan of Kimberly's Sainthood was accepted far and wide but the issue remained; was she the Child of God, the half-sister of Jesus? Heresy or divinity? The whole issue became moot when it was learned that Jesus would visit her soon after he visited the Pope, Christ's Vicar on Earth.

Unknown to Kim, her followers and Samuel, were hard at work getting ready to publish, "The Epistle of Saint Kimberly." The Pope had seen a draft and had granted his important imprimatur.

A new flag was proposed for America. The new 54-star flag had a red Maltese Cross on a circular white field in center of the blue canton containing 54 stars arranged in 3 sets of three on either side of the circle and four rows of nine stars above and below the circle. The 13 red and white stripes are unchanged. Discussions about the new "Christian flag" along with debates about whether the Ten Commandments should be adopted as part of the U.S. Constitutions were ongoing. The new states eagerly waited for confirmation.

Jesus returned to Jerusalem from the clouds above….in Kimberly's Gulfstream III private jet. The distinctive Templar cross on the fuselage was known to one and all so a crowd quickly gathered. Those in the know thought, "Of course."

When the door-stairs opened, four men in suits exited, the one with a derby hat and cigar came down first. Two stood on each side of the stairs and went to full Archangel mode, halos, wings, golden breastplates, and the whole dress kit. Then, having their divinity firmly established, came Jesus followed by Kim to a cheering audience. Jesus leaned over and whispered to Kim,"Remember the reception that I received on what they now call "Palm Sunday. A few days later I was on the cross"

Kim, smiled and said, "But you did not have Samuel, Gabriel, Michael, and Raphael at your back. Remember, you told your followers that they could tread among snakes and go unharmed? I have the same guarantee for you, honored elder brother."

Jesus had a nice visit after he and Kim had declared, and enforced, a 20-foot circle past which
paparazzi and overeager videographers could not
pass. They enjoyed a passover meal at the finest res-
taurant in town with a limited guest list and played
tourist at Nazareth, Capernaum, Bethlehem, and
Jerusalem. Jesus kept muttering "This isn't right"
when shown this and that "Holy Site" but He kept a
smile on his face and said nothing out loud. A foot
or two or a mile or three made no difference if the
object of reverence was sincere. The where was not
as important as the what of it.

As they took off, Jesus said, "What next Sis? And,
by the way, your Diet Cokes are pretty good. The
only thing that we had in the old days that was re-
liably safe to drink was wine and that was pretty
variable."

"Well, Brother, I thought that we might drop in
on Glenview to let you get to know some of your
relatives. We also have a bear on a column that I
am particularly fond of. We will visit him to say hel-
lo. And, since Passover is celebrated in April these
days, you might have a chance to experience snow.

And, so the brother and sister got to know and
appreciate each other before they went their separate ways to fulfill their destinies and that of their
Father.

figure 4:
Hug the Bear
Glenview, IL

figure 5:
previous books available from
amazon.com in book or kindle format